"Sandra . . . please." She seethed in anxious anticipation. Unrepentant, and in slow deliberation, Sandra kissed Karen's throat and neck and nibbled at her shoulder again. With her left hand now working in concert with Karen's buttocks, Sandra kneaded Karen's flesh into a wanton, thrusting obsession. The sweet teasing torture continued, annihilating all vestiges of inhibitions or illusion of resistance. Sweat covered Karen's throat, ran between her breasts, and mingled with the wet curls of hair between her legs. She fell back onto the bed as she pulled Sandra down with her. Her legs wrapped high around Sandra's body as she exposed her need to thrust eagerly against the obliging hand.

About the Author

Janet McClellan began her career in law enforcement at the tender age of nineteen. She worked for more than twenty-six years in various aspects of criminal justice, including patrol officer, undercover investigator, detective, college professor, and prisons systems manager/administrator in various parts of the country. At forty-five she returned to law enforcement as the police chief for a small town in Kansas.

Penn Valley PHOENIX

Janet McClellan

THE NAIAD PRESS, INC.
1998

Printed in the United States of America on acid-free paper
First Edition

Editor: Lila Empson
Cover designer: Bonnie Liss (Phoenix Graphics)
Typesetter: Sandi Stancil

Library of Congress Cataloging-in-Publication Data

McClellan, Janet, 1951 –
   Penn Valley Phoenix : a Tru North mystery / by
Janet McClellan.
      p.   cm.
   ISBN 1-56280-200-3
   I. Title.
PS3563.C3413P46   1997
813'.54—dc21

97-40427
CIP

To K. W.
You know who you are.

Acknowledgment

To the women of Naiad,
as always, my sincerest thanks.

Chapter 1

Karen Bayborn slipped off her robe. She lowered her shapely legs over the edge and into the bubbling turmoil of the Jacuzzi. She gasped and caught her breath, as the churning madness of the bubbles played teasingly at her buttocks and lapped suggestively against her pubic hairs. Closing her eyes, she sank into the scalding surprise of the swirling water and willed herself to be still enough to let her body adjust to the temperature. The Jacuzzi consumed a sixth of the fenced garden apartment's postage-stamp yard. Space was not the issue. The

Jacuzzi was a comfort, a luxury, and a gift from her lover.

The warm winds of the mid-June night teased at the bun she'd fashioned of her long brown hair, whipping the strands loose to lie in wet ringlets against her neck. Over the sky the distant sounds of city traffic buzzed like perturbed bees on honey-foraging parties.

Karen opened her eyes and gazed into the shrouded sky. The cap of night was held brightly at bay by city lights. It was ten o'clock, and she had to wait. Her lover would not call until after midnight. Karen would have to content herself with longing, desire, and fantasy until it was safe to go, when the other had left and she could belong to Sandra for a few precious hours or a few precious days. It would be worth the wait. In the beginning, she hadn't known she was waiting or what she'd been waiting for.

Memory beckoned, whispered to her in her languishing vigil of anticipation. As she waited for the call, her name flitted through her mind — Sandra, Sandra. It floated on her mind and, with the breeze of warm June air, contrived to make her heart surge with joy.

She remembered the first time she'd been introduced to Sandra Vandamier and the intensity of the eyes that had swept over her. Hooded, suggestive, provocative eyes that carelessly glanced at her and then her résumé. That had been four months ago. A lifetime, a bewitching turning point.

No one can know, she mused. It might have happened some other time, some other place, to some other person, or she might have missed it entirely. But no one can know that it will happen or that it will bring truth with it when it does. She had not guessed before. Could not have imagined. Or she'd avoided it as a possibility while she clung to other expectations, standard requirements, neat and tidy observations and behaviors.

It had been meticulous, unexpected, and stirring — all of that and all at the same time. She was Sandra and the unexpected. She had brought with her the point of knowing. Without having ever consciously guessed or conjured, Karen had not known before that she could ever love a woman. The wondrous woman's name was Sandra. Karen knew her introduction to this longing and knowledge, which only another woman could have shown her, had to happen. The secrets had broken open like a fragile piñata in celebration of rebirth and renewal, and all the lovely treats had fallen sweetly at her feet.

Karen replayed the memory for herself. She had arrived at the restaurateur's office in response to a newspaper advertisement indicating that Phoebe's Phoenix was looking for a new hostess. She had risked applying because she was bored with her waitress job at Avenue Landing. At Avenue Landing there had been no hope of advancement, better tips, or more engaging pieces of the business pie. The owner/operator couple performed the management, bookkeeping, and hostess/host duties themselves. They were stingy with their compliments to staff, and they did not share the credit or benefit of their steadily improving enterprise.

At twenty-nine Karen hoped for more, better, and

sooner. She wanted an opportunity to practice what she had learned in the restaurant business and an opportunity to learn more.

Her dream had been to save her money or to find a wealthy backer to support the first lean year of public scrutiny reserved for all new ventures attempted in the Westport area of Kansas City, Missouri.

She knew she had proved her willingness to learn from the bottom up by putting in arduous hours for eight years in restaurants throughout Kansas City. She'd schooled herself and took classes in business and restaurant management at Penn Valley Junior College. She didn't want to wait her whole life for her big break to come. Impatience and the need to test her wings made her search the want ads weekly.

Sandra Vandamier was the break Karen had been waiting for. She had heard about Vandamier, the manager and controlling partner of Phoebe's Phoenix. Karen had also heard about the sexual appetites attributed to the forty-five-year-old woman. Rumors floated freely regarding Vandamier's sleekness, firm body, and exotic passions. It was hard to have too many secrets in the multifaceted world of Kansas City's nightlife. For the climbing and upwardly-scratching mobile, there were only so many places to go, so many who would be seen, so much to share and imagine.

Light or bright, closed or closeted, the city and its splendid assortment of conservative and alternative communities were connected in her work by the tendrils of tantalizing tales. Fact or fiction. Reality or illusion. The conversations, whispers, and questions bubbled up to the surface of imaginations and conversations as freely as heated water comes to boil.

Karen had heard the stories, but she did not let the rumors or facts distract her from her goal or keep her from her quest. Karen saw it as simply a matter of "whatever it takes" to get her where she wanted to go. At first, it had simply been that she'd paid in kind or fact or whatever it cost to get ahead. She had not anticipated everything else because she'd not defined it for herself.

Vandamier's eyes had explored her, tantalized her suggestively, and assaulted her with an intense interview meant to test her knowledge and mettle. It was a rigorous grilling. Vandamier had appraised her for the tact, courtesy, and civility required of hostesses in upscale restaurants. In this business there could be no flinching, no hesitation, and no loss of courtesy or control. The moneyed clients did not like bad manners, bad service, or bad management of their time. An incompetent host or hostess would have a direct effect on the profit and success of a restaurant. A hostess was expected to be all things to the clients, staff, and interests of the management. The satisfaction of the customer and the favorable reputation of a restaurant was the requirement.

Phoebe's Phoenix was located three blocks north of Westport and was snuggled up against the rolling edge of what once was the high, terraced glen known as Penn Valley. The original swelling roll of gentle bluffs had long been obscured by the crowding homes, parks, streets, shopping areas, and community college of the same name. In a not so distant past it had been an ethnic community comprising French and

Lithuanians, Slavs, and miscellaneous other Eastern Europeans. By the late sixties, the ethnicity had shifted to the people bearing Spanish surnames — Mexican Americans, Latinos, or Chicanos, depending on one's political consciousness.

Most of the customers who came to Phoebe's Phoenix and were familiar with Penn Valley or the Westport area didn't refer to the restaurant as Phoebe's Phoenix. For whatever reason, the combination of words and sound proved to be too difficult or perplexing. So it became known simply as the Phoenix, and its reputation under the care and guidance of Sandra Vandamier blazed across the sky of Kansas City like its legendary name.

During the last six years, the new co-owner had also blazed her own wide swath through the notable and less notable nightlife of the city. Sandra Vandamier was known to be demanding, exacting, domineering, and seductive of and to those in whom she took an interest. Her reputation as an extraordinary restaurateur spread like fire through the underground.

"Whatever it takes," Karen had told herself on the long drive to the restaurant. She maintained that concentrated and determined echo in the back of her mind throughout the interview. "Whatever it takes," she chanted under Vandamier's imposing scrutiny. She wouldn't know that her courage and audacity became part of her charm for Sandra.

It had taken a second and third interview to land the job. After the formal office interview, a second interview was held at a club across town. Sandra Vandamier had told Karen to meet her at the

Phoenix and to be prepared to have dinner, dressed appropriately, and to be evaluated again. Vandamier had then returned her to her current place of employment at the Avenue Landing. Later, Karen realized that the test had begun by the naming of the place.

It was professionally incautious to allow oneself to be seen with the competition, and Vandamier was direct competition with Avenue Landing. Phoebe's Phoenix had been engaged in a hot war with Avenue Landing for the same high rollers, and the Landing had been losing all but the most minor skirmishes. But Vandamier appeared comfortable conducting tests with stress twists added to them. It had been cruel for Vandamier to have Karen risk her only source of income without the slightest promise of a replacement. It was the first occasion for Karen to learn about the mild streak of sadism that would surface in Vandamier, but it would not be the last. Karen would come to know how that twist in her employer/lover could turn Sandra to feral behavior.

The interview at Avenue Landing had consisted of Vandamier requesting that Karen observe, report, and discuss the appropriate and inappropriate operations of the restaurant with her. Karen found herself engaged in the tactical analysis of the bombarding minutia of the dinnertime crowd where waiters, waitresses, and host were deployed to one skirmish and then another. Vandamier had appeared pleased with Karen's wit, analysis, and critical eye. An invitation for a third interview was offered.

The last interview had been conducted later that evening at Vandamier's home. Karen believed she was

7

being invited to Vandamier's house to be given a congratulatory drink and to hear the conditions of employment and the terms of compensation. She had not known nor guessed the extent of willfulness Vandamier possessed.

It began cordially enough. A snifter of fine brandy, gently warmed by Vandamier's hands, along with easy conversation. The chill of the March air was warmed by a roaring fire in the sumptuous den. Soft classical music floated through the room, and the lights were turned low. Alto and soprano voices fell sweetly on Karen's ear, and she was lulled into a sense of relaxation at the end of the evening's exhausting interview. Conversation with Vandamier seemed to flow effortlessly.

Talking of the vision Vandamier held for the prosperity of the restaurant, Karen watched her soon-to-be new employer with growing admiration and an interest she could not yet name. She noticed the turn of Sandra Vandamier's neck, the languid way she moved, the clinging sweep of fabric on her thigh, and the careful poses Vandamier offered. Karen felt herself curiously drawn to her as she moved to stand nearer the flickering fire.

Vandamier's eyes were heavy and shadowed in the indirect lighting. Nothing was indirect about the temptation, inclination, or suggestion residing there, however. Her large brown eyes bespoke the question and taunted Karen to respond. Inquiry and sensuousness were mixed in a heady combination as Sandra asked about Karen's life. They danced the fine and gentle dance of possibilities and innuendo around the elegant furniture, close to the fire, and then away again into the shadowed room. Tingling skin and

8

fascination not even whispered drew them together like moths to a flame. Power courted desire, and the knowing suggestion of experience tempted the uninitiated.

Sandra Vandamier reached for Karen and her hand grazed her right breast as it rose to stroke the curve of Karen's jaw. Karen turned her face into the full caress of that hand as she let her lips gently press against Sandra's thumb. Her lips lingered as Sandra traced the bottom lip and circled up to its winged upper mate. A flick of her tongue and Karen tasted the scent of perfume mixed with a vanishing hint of salt.

Sandra pressed her thumb forward and parted Karen's lips. Karen breathed in her luxurious scent and swayed in the spell they were weaving. Sandra stayed her thumb's tease and joined it with eager lips. Warm mouths met, breathed hot, and pressed against each other in teasing wetness. Freeing her thumb, Sandra stroked Karen's arm, captured her waist, and urged her closer. She reached around, found the curve of Karen's buttocks, touched the arching rise of her back, and caressed her gently up to her shoulders. Tightness and passion overtook them. Locked in the embrace, they rushed toward a primal shore.

They stood back from each other, and the walls reflected their skirted silhouettes in the dancing lights cast by the fire. A sign, a suggestion, and the surrender signaled a beginning in the late winter's night. Sandra slipped a hand into Karen's and led her toward the secluded bedroom. Karen followed in a captivated haze.

The bed was queen-size. A luxury of satin,

pillows, and lace. The back of Karen's calves touched the cool spread as Sandra's eyes searched her face. Karen wanted to look away, to break contact with the intensity of those eyes, but she didn't dare. It would have meant losing contact with what she wanted. It seemed as though she'd been hungry all her life and had never been fed, that she'd been thirsty without hope of having her thirst slaked.

Sandra closed her eyes as she brought her hands up under Karen's breasts to seize and squeeze them tenderly. Her hands stroked Karen's ribs in gratifying titillation, and then moved down to the soft bend of her waist and down to the rounding of her hips. A tremble passed under her hands, and she sensed an untapped desire stir in Karen.

Karen reached through the darkness and wrapped her arms around Sandra's neck. Sandra's lips met hers, her tongue gliding between Karen's lips and teasing flickeringly inside. Teeth gently nipped her bottom lip and sucked the pouting mound. Karen's breath escaped from her like a plea.

Their tongues met, and Sandra sucked her in, darting her tongue sharply and suggestively against Karen's teeth and tongue. She held her with a long, succulent search that made Karen rise against her in an arch of desire. Karen did not know where she was or what she wanted.

"I've . . . not," Karen struggled to explain without excuse, unwilling to end it, not wanting it to stop.

"Yes," Sandra's voice responded in the freedom of Karen's gasp. "But you want to. Want to now, don't you, dear?" There was no hurry in the words. They were paced like a suggestion that knows its own time. She held Karen and let her mouth brand hot kisses down Karen's lovely neck to the hollow of her throat and sear across her shoulder.

"I . . . god, yes."

"Goddess," Sandra corrected.

Sandra was there in the flames of Karen's emerging desire and with her in its increase. Intensely there. Commandingly there. Karen relented and let Sandra take from her the precious little resistance she had mustered. Sandra drove it wordlessly from her in the sweep of desire. Again Karen hesitated but was distracted from her thoughts by the darting tongue that sought her. There were no more words. Nothing intelligible slipped between them and their desire.

Sandra's impassioned full-body contact tilted Karen gently back. Sandra's hands slipped the zipper down from the back collar to the tip of Karen's spine, and reached through the opened dress to run her hands across the freshly-bared flesh. One hand coaxed the shoulders of the dress to slip away from their precarious perch. Karen let it slide to the floor, making sure the searching tongue would not escape her mouth. A delicious fire burned in her, making her knees ineffective under her.

"Ohhnnn — oughn!" She heard herself pleading yet melted under the touch as Sandra pulled the half-slip off to roughly caress Karen's taut buttocks. Karen gasped. Sandra's left hand held her while the right grazed her stomach and pressed hard between her legs. Karen felt her need rising hotly into that hand as it explored the wetness of the flimsy silk lace. She opened her legs at the persistent urging tease of Sandra's fingertips that pulled temptingly at the edges of the lace. Karen pressed into the hand to demand more.

"Sandra . . . please." She seethed in anxious anticipation. Unrepentant, and in slow deliberation, Sandra kissed Karen's throat and neck and nibbled at her shoulder again. With her left hand now working in concert with Karen's buttocks, Sandra kneaded Karen's flesh into a wanton, thrusting obsession. The sweet teasing torture continued, annihilating all vestiges of inhibitions or illusion of resistance. Sweat covered Karen's throat, ran between her breasts, and mingled with the wet curls of hair between her legs. She fell back onto the bed as she pulled Sandra down with her. Her legs wrapped high around Sandra's body as she exposed her need to thrust eagerly against the obliging hand.

Karen answered the call from deep within. A voice soft and longing, wild and untamed. A call she'd never heard before.

Sandra raised herself and smiled down at Karen as she grabbed the silk panties to drag them from Karen's hips. A dusky, sweet aroma rose to fill her nostrils, and she inhaled the fragrance of passion. Her hand returned to seek the soft, inviting wetness. Leaning over her quarry, she let her mouth seek Karen's lips and her fingers slip through the blond curls to the readied ripeness.

Karen's body spasmodically erupted in unabashed need. Her hips sought the rhythm singing deep within her. Sandra's fingers pulled in and out, serving her need and spilling their magic into her. Karen felt herself thundering down dark-tossed waves, drowning in suboceanic tides only to writhe on the crest of Sandra's probing fingers. Karen struggled, bucked, and reared from the bed. She gasped in ragged breaths and surged again and again until she floated through a precious calm. A rapacious void swallowed her, and she subsided in her need. A sudden flicking of Sandra's fingers and thrusting of her hand sent Karen back over the edge to the self-same zenith from which she'd fallen. The aching, needful tide washed her up on the beach of a new country in her soul.

Her passions at peace, breath catching in her throat, and sobs quietly breaking through, Karen's body was no longer interested in willful movement. A soft, urging voice distantly asked, "Do you want the rest?"

"The rest?" she asked incredulously. "There's more?"

"Much more."

"More?" The only word Karen could find.

The implied disbelief roused Sandra, and Karen was led to the promise of more.

Suddenly, the phone next to Karen's head rang viciously, causing her to start in surprise and strike her head on the rounded lip of the Jacuzzi. She grabbed for the phone and her head simultaneously. The intrusion had knocked her out of her reverie and almost knocked her out. Whoever was on the other end of the line would be made to understand her wrath.

"What," she said, all but screaming into the phone.

"Karen?" Sandra's warm tones asked.

"Sandra, is that you?"

"Of course. Why do you sound so cross?"

"It's . . . it's nothing. I banged my head getting to the phone. What time is it?"

"It's eleven, dear. Why don't you come over?"

"What about Diana?"

"She left for the airport. But that's a long story. Come on over," Sandra urged.

"It will take me a few minutes. I fell asleep in the Jacuzzi," Karen admitted.

"Even better. You'll be deliciously flawless, warmed to the bone, and luscious. I can hardly wait."

"I'll just shower and change."

"Don't change a thing for me."

"I'll see you in about an hour."

"Don't make me wait too long. You know I hate to be kept waiting," Sandra said with unveiled threat. She'd been slowly and meticulously working to possess Karen. Sandra had practiced a loosening of all of Karen's inhibitions to bring her under her dominance and control. It was a game of skill and desire. It was an orchestrated game Sandra played like a maestro.

"I know," Karen muttered. "But I feel like a prune, and I want you to be pleased with me."

"I'll be here, dear. I'll be patient. Just this once," Sandra said as she hung up.

Karen looked at the phone and sighed heavily. She was determined to take her time showering. She

14

knew that Sandra would be upset if she didn't properly prepare for her.

"Whatever it takes," she said as she climbed out of the bubbling water and trotted back inside the apartment.

Chapter 2

The telephone rang, and Tru North reached over to pick it up. She yelled into the receiver. It kept ringing and ringing in her ear. She looked at it perplexedly and said hello again while it rang in her hand. In frustration, she roared her name at the menace. When no one responded, she slammed it down. Dementedly, it kept ringing and ringing.

She struggled in her sleep, jerking awake as the telephone on the nightstand clamored for her attention. Rolling across the bed, she reached out to grab the infernal machine.

"North," she said in the rasping irritated tones of sleep.

"Turn on a light, sit up, and get a pencil," Bob Jones directed her.

"I am awake," Tru protested as she pulled the sheet up closer to her neck and tried to ignore him.

"Like hell," he teased. "Anyway, get yourself down to 8395 Summitt Parkway Villas."

"Why should I?"

"'Cause I'm your immediate supervisor, and it's your turn on the wheel."

"Homicide?"

"From what I can get, it's more like a botched burglary or lover's quarrel. The first officer at the scene is a year out of academy, so who knows."

"Great." Tru sat up, turned on the light, and searched for a pen to write down the address that Jones had given her. There was no paper near the phone, so she wrote the address on the palm of her left hand, like a grade-school cheat sheet.

"Yeah, well, that's the way it goes. But, it's yours ole girl. Bates and Garvan will second you."

"I'm not an ole girl —" Tru started. "Gregory Bates? For the love of sanity, Bob, he just came up from checks and sex. He's a politico on short tenure if his police patron-parson has his way. Give him to somebody else," Tru complained as she pitched back the bedcovers and wandered into the bathroom with the cordless phone.

"He's yours. That's the way Captain Rhonn wanted it. Tom Garvan is the best I can do for an apology. Every boy needs his mother," Bob said, chuckling as he hung up.

Tru stared in dismay at her phone and almost

slammed it on the ceramic sink. She hesitated, punched off the TALK button instead, and laid it down gently. She didn't want her anger to break her phone.

Captain Rhonn, "the Wrath of Rhonn," had been a royal pain in the ass since assuming command of the division the year before. During the initial months of his tenure, he'd seen to it that three detectives were either retired early or quietly dismissed. He was part of the new breed of management. They talked softly and carried a howitzer. They were practiced at using all the right words, and they refrained from sexist or ethnic slander and covered their biases and prejudices with stupefying ease. They still had all the same prejudices the old guard held, but they'd been schooled and trained to hide them under phrases like *organizational necessity*, *for the good of the order*, and something about *economic necessity*. Their sleekness made them more dangerous than the rubes they had replaced. They were problematic for the troops. You could always tell a shark by its fin, but barracudas gave no warning short of the kill. Barracudas were sleek, had smaller teeth, and needed only desire, not blood, to draw them to a likely victim.

Captain Rhonn, Tru knew, had targeted her for his fourth successful termination. She had managed to slide by it by concluding an investigation and receiving the favor of upper administration several months ago. Now, he was deciding whom he'd team her with, even though Jones was the unit supervisor. Bates was a snitch, carrier of tales, and eager liar if the truth would not serve him. It meant that the

18

war between Rhonn and Tru was not over yet. It had simply stalled for halftime maneuvering.

Shit, she thought ruefully. Gregory Bates. At thirty-two he was a favored child of one of the commissioners. He was a debt due for payment in the top rungs of the police hierarchy. He was the organizational child of that commissioner-cum-patron-parson. And he was a real danger. Fast-tracker, short-timer, incompetent, swaggering braggart and insider snitch. Nobody in the agency wanted him. No one in the unit wanted him. They simply had to endure him until his patron booted him farther along and up the ladder. They were grooming and preparing him for his big desk at administrative headquarters. Thus far, his longest tenure had been as a patrol officer, and that for only three years. He'd spent the last four years traipsing through the various divisions and units like some daddy's boy. Four months here, six months there. During his past two months in homicide, Jones had managed to assign him the safe suicides and a few domestic murders. Nothing serious, taxing, or too easy to screw up. And now he belonged to Tru because Captain Rhonn could dictate terms. Rhonn was inclined to dictate whenever he felt pushed, pressed, or uncertain. It was a trick for weak men. And in the unit, Rhonn was the weak link.

Tru stumbled to the closet and threw on a pair of slacks and a cotton shirt. Going to the bathroom, she hurriedly combed her hair, washed the sleep from her eyes, and brushed her teeth as she hoped fervently that Garvan would be the saving grace Jones had promised. Grabbing her briefcase and jacket, she dashed out the door.

Getting into her car, Tru slammed the magnetic red strobe to the roof and sped across town. Summitt Parkway Villas was a recent addition to the metropolitan area. Seven years earlier the developer had built fine large homes surrounded by manicured lawns with handsome privacy fences surrounded by battalions of tiny trees. The houses were laid out backed up to a golf course to give the impression and protection of space. A planned community. Selective, private and, until tonight, supposedly crime free. Number 8395 sat at the wide end of a roaming cul-de-sac, farthest from the reaches of the roadway and in the center of its two-acre lot.

By the time she arrived, the flashing lights of patrol cars and an ambulance and the red beanies of unmarked vehicles were crowded at the drive in front of the house. She parked her car a hundred feet back from the seeming traffic jam and pulled out the Minicam from her briefcase. She checked to make sure the film was fresh and unused before turning it on the lighted scene in front of her. Tru scanned the area with the lens, focusing on the tight little knots of people on the outside of the cordoned area. People wearing housecoats, pajamas, and classy nightshirts.

She walked forward. One eye minded the shots while the other watched where she was going. She panned cars, license plates, and other houses. Without the film, she might forget the details of the night, the way the sky looked, the temperature, the humidity, the people, or some other peculiar detail that might prove to be the break in the case. Closer in, she zoomed to faces, then took a long shot back at her car and the front of the house at wide angle

20

to get perspective. She snapped the camera off and walked up to the officer at the door.

"Are Bates and Garvan here?"

"Went in about ten minutes ago," the young uniformed officer responded.

She brushed past him and then stopped. "Did you get here first?"

"Yeah," the officer said dejectedly. "We also serve who stand and wait."

"That's right, you do." Her tone reminded the officer that departmental policy demanded the first officer on the scene of a possible homicide to secure the scene, check for survivors or perpetrators, and secure witnesses or suspects. But never, never were they supposed to investigate, touch, move, rearrange, or damage the crime scene. It was tough duty. Homicides were considered the sexiest detail imaginable by patrol officers until they actually got an assignment to the sentry duty and real task of noninvolvement.

Inside the house, the assistant lab photographer directed Tru from the foyer up the stairs to the second floor. As Tru bounded up the stairs, she took the tape recorder from her jacket pocket and attached the tiny microphone to her lapel near her throat. It would give her an opportunity to keep her hands free while whispering notes, observations, suggestions, and names of personnel at the scene. She whispered her first impressions into the mike.

She had started carrying the recording device several months ago. She experimented at first, wondering whether or not it would be too intrusive. It hadn't been. No one had noticed the small black cord against her customary double-breasted dark jacket. The microphone was generally taken for a lapel pin, an accessory, or other adornment.

Bob Jones had started to kid her about talking to herself while they were picking up the pieces of people and processes at the scene of an attempted daylight robbery of a downtown gun and ammo supplier. She had been walking the perimeter, noting blood splatters, bloody pools, and trajectories of spent bullets against the statements provided by the owners. Trying to rob a gun and ammo store had to be one of the dumbest things Tru had heard of anyone attempting. The owners had blazed away at the robbers. The result had been quick and final for the hooded men. When the smoke cleared, it was Robbers 0 – Store Owners 2. The tape recorder had proved itself useful and she kept it as part of her investigative equipment.

At the Summitt address, Tru walked down the wide hallway noticing the flowers on the tables and soft pastel oils tastefully marching against the walls. The house and its location, design, and neighborhood spoke of new money. But inside, Tru observed the quiet reserved enunciation of either good taste or old money. It didn't brag. Rather, it spoke of owners who knew who they were and who did not require the flash or overreaching garishness so often associated with first-generation prosperity. Tru wondered if the tastes were earned or learned.

Walking past an adjacent bedroom, Tru saw a young woman sitting on the bed weeping softly to herself. Tru stopped and gazed through the door at her. The clear, unblemished skin and general demeanor made her look very young, vulnerable, and alone.

Child, witness, spouse, suspect, accidental interloper, the possibilities ran through Tru's mind. She didn't know who she was yet, but for Tru the young woman belonged to one of the five categories. The trick was to find out which one.

The young woman's long legs were tucked to one side as she leaned against the tall bedpost for support. Tru thought she looked childlike and lost in her grief. Then she saw the blood smudges on her hands, a grazing of the same on the side of her right cheek, and a dark stain on her blouse. Tru knew the young woman had touched the victim but did not assign her to a specific category. Yet.

She looked up at Tru. The long brown hair fell away from her face. Her blue eyes were large, distantly alive, and red rimmed. The sorrow and anguish in those eyes did nothing to diminish the loveliness Tru saw hiding inside them. She nodded briskly to the young woman and returned to the hallway.

A cluster of uniformed officers and milling lab techs signaled the room Tru was looking for. She walked in and saw Gregory Bates leaning over the body as Tom Garvan directed a lab tech to get prints from the bedroom and adjoining bathroom. Bates had a lopsided grin on his face that appeared to herald the beginning of a leer. Tru breathed in deeply through her nose, trying to keep herself calm and controlled. For Tru, it was one thing to be forced into the position of being a voyeur to death, but it was another matter to have the look of someone who liked it. She made a mental note of the leering grin on Bates's face.

"Bates," Tru commanded.

"North," he flinched, but responded without looking up.

"Over here, Bates," Tru motioned to him. He stood up and met her eyes, his forehead crinkled in perplexity. "What?"

"Find out," Tru insisted and turned from him to walk to the other side of the generous room. His frown turned to a scowl as he followed her.

"What?"

"Did you talk to the first officer on the scene? Have you walked through the rest of the house? Have you had any uniforms go talk to the neighbors? Have you touched, moved, breathed on, or otherwise screwed anything else up in this room?" Tru snapped off the words at him in a confidentially quiet but direct rapid-fire voice.

Bates's face flushed, then the revealing red crept up his neck. His mouth opened several times, fish-wise, and closed again. He swiveled his head toward Garvan, who pointedly ignored him.

"Well?" Tru insisted.

"No, but Captain Rhonn said —" he began.

"Rhonn said you were an assist. An assist in this case, the next case, and any other we might have the misfortune of sharing. That means you don't go stumbling through the scene, poking, prodding, or even breathing on victims until someone lets you."

"But —"

"The only *but* is the one you have attached to you as you get back down those stairs and walk this one through by the book. Got it?" Tru said, barely containing her irritation. She heard Garvan cough lightly. Out of the corner of her eye she saw his quick slanted grin as he spoke to the tech.

"I —"

"You know the routine, don't you, Bates? There're the assigned investigators and their assistant backups. You're an untried back. So, you back way up and do what you're told to do. And don't you dare jump into my space unless you're invited."

"You don't —" he began ineffectually.

"No," Tru said, dropping her voice to a whisper. "You don't embarrass yourself. This is no place to challenge me. There is no way to win, and you wouldn't want to screw anything up here, now would you? It might keep you from becoming chief before you're forty-five." Her eyes narrowed in reproach.

At six-foot-two he towered over her five-foot-five height as he looked down into her dark gray eyes. He didn't like what he found there. Tru wasn't known for her sense of humor in the unit. Her small, svelte body belied her strength. He was two years younger and had eighty pounds on her. He faltered. He'd heard stories and wondered what and how much might be fact.

She wasn't loved by command, but she was grudgingly respected. It was common knowledge or myth of the department that she could fall into a barrel of shit and still come out smelling like a rose. He knew no officer could do that without having some protection from above. Bates debated whether or not she also had a guardian patron hiding and watching at headquarters. He knew it was best not to mess with someone's kid, just in case her big-ugly had a bigger baton than his did.

He swallowed hard and let the anger flow back down his throat to land at the bottom of his empty stomach. "Yes, ma'am," he said as he turned on his heel and left the room.

"Don't be too hard on the boy," Tom Garvan said as he walked over to Tru. Garvan looked older than his forty-three years. His slightly sagging shoulders and hangdog expression, accentuated by the deep, tanned creases in his face, exaggerated his appearance of advanced age. The cheap suit only added to the picture.

"Boy? Boil on my tush is more like it," Tru countered, and shook it off. "Who is she?" Tru nodded in the direction of the body.

Garvan flipped open his notebook. "The deceased is one Sandra Vandamier, age forty-five. She was found like this by the young woman in the other room, a Karen Bayborn. How do you want to do this?"

"The *K. C. Star*'s 'Inside Edition' wealthy, restaurant-owning Sandra Vandamier? Great. By the numbers and back again. I see television in our future and gnashing of teeth downtown on this one. You agree?"

"You think this is *crimson crime*? I was kinda hoping to pull a *blue speck,*" he said, using the department's coded words. The unit had long ago dubbed *crimson crimes* as the hair-pulling dead-end crimes — or the ones that made the public scream for quick closure. *Blue specks* were easier-to-solve, routine murders and garden-variety deaths. Officers and detectives generally abbreviated the terms to simply *red* or *blue*. *Red* for the public's blood pressure and the aggravation they caused; *blue* for the poor sap who fell within the normal specter of unattended or wrongful death.

"Tom, every time I think blue it goes red on me," Tru said as she walked over to the far side of the bed where the body lay in the contours of the last efforts of life. She had mid-length dark brown hair and glazed brown eyes. She had been large breasted, but those once beautiful features were now marred by a seeping hole in her chest. A gun lay close to her outstretched right hand. Her lavender silk-and-brocade night slip had twisted when she'd fallen. Its length had pulled up to lie across her partially exposed thighs. She had been striking. A tall, manicured appearance with the sleekness that professed attention to detail radiated from the supine body. All of that, and money too. Tru looked on in wonder at the artless death that had taken Vandamier.

Over the years Tru had come to believe that death was art. The final touch and end of a portrait drawn through the years. It didn't sum the life, condemn it, applaud it, or void it. It was simply the last stroke. Tru believed that if death was art, then so too was the investigation of death an art unto itself. Not a pen or brush to be taken up by the timid, the immature, or the amateur. It was a questing for answers as surely as any other form of contemplation or meditation. But it was messier. It exposed victims, families, friends, lovers, onlookers, and investigators to the full range of human response. It pulled up the full spectrum of human psychology replete with its often disavowed needs, passions, desires, and explosive exhibitions. It was messier because sometimes the things that human beings did to themselves and one another were more squalid than most people would have guessed or preferred them to be.

Tru gazed at the picture of death before her. Her eyes moved in wider and wider circles from the center of that picture to take in the full context and contents of the room. She looked for composition, disposition, sequence, and form in the abstraction of death. In life and in death every picture would tell a story. And every story had to have its beginning, a middle, and an end. This one would be no different, except as it had played itself out in Vandamier's life.

Tru heard the fleeting tumble of questions pummeling around in her head. Why this? Why is the body here and not somewhere else? Why was it done this way? Was this what was intended or is this a penumbra shadowing the light? If this is the picture, what is wrong with it and what is right? What did the artist of this death do, not do, take out, leave in, or leave behind? What were the thoughts or mad dreams of the one who made this death?

Tru called Tom Garvan back to her side and quickly told him what she'd like to have done to the room. He nodded, noting those that he'd previously directed the techs to do. She agreed and asked for completeness. He underscored her requests, made suggestions, and received her acknowledgments.

She asked for five Polaroid pictures of the body taken from various angles to the bed. She wanted to have the pictures fresh and accessible for her scrutiny after the pathologist removed the body. Tru told him she didn't want the body moved until the photographs were made.

"Is that a witness or suspect down the hall?" Tru asked.

"Ms. Karen Bayborn. According to her, she arrived after midnight and found the victim like this. Bayborn was the one who called it in. But I don't know yet which side of the fence she's on." Garvan never jumped to conclusions any more than Tru.

"Know anything about her?"

"Bates tried to talk to her, but he gave up when she started crying again."

"What did he ask her?"

"Something about if she saw it happen, saw the victim put the gun to her chest. Wanted to know if she got the blood on her from the muzzle splatters." Tom looked at Tru and winced.

"I think we're going to need to read the psych profile on our new partner, Mr. Bates, wouldn't you say?" Tru asked as she shook her head in consternation.

"I don't like wading in garbage," Tom declined.

"Let's just say that we probably need to. If his line of questioning is any indication, either he has no bedside manner or there are some proclivities that might not be suitable for homicide and its ready availability of dead bodies."

"A guess. Are you trying to tell me you don't like him?"

"A guess and yes. Just put it under your hat and let's keep an eye on him. OK?"

"You know it's a little kinky to suggest that he

might be a ghoul perp. Do such suspicions mean we should look at your psych profile, too?" Garvan had a lazy approach to his work, but that laziness was a skillful disguise for a quick mind. He'd run into officers who had a morbid fascination with death. Sometimes the fascination took on sexual overtones. The warning bells were present with Bates, but he wanted to counter Tru's aroused concern with humor so she could rethink the idea.

"Only if you're not frightened of your fantasies," Tru taunted. Tru had worked with Garvan before. He was steady and conscientious and engaged in the light banter of the reserved. There were times when light banter was the only saving grace one could afford while staring at the unattractive aftermath of human interactions.

"Be still, my beating heart," Tom Garvan countered in his habitual nasal tones.

No one on the department wanted to discuss their psychological profiles or ever would. It was bad enough that the shrinks hired by the department might keep them on file. Tru never asked about hers. She considered it fair enough that the department had hired her without recriminations after she'd taken the test back in her academy days. To be hired as a permanent party the profile would have had to contain what the psychologists would consider the necessary balance of assertiveness, inquisitiveness, emotional control, and propensity toward honesty and integrity. There was an allowable range of peculiarities. And, whatever those mysterious statistical variances were, the department knew Tru and the other officers had at one time fallen within that allowance. There would be no need to take another psychological evaluation. No need, unless the administration suspected that some line had been crossed or some presumed level of normalcy had been breached.

Chapter 3

Tru walked down the hall toward the bedroom she'd seen Karen Bayborn in. The medical examiner and his assistant were trudging past her. They struggled under the weight of their bags, instruments, and lighting. Seeing them, Tru knew there would now be further indignities heaped on the body of the victim.

As a first step, a rectal thermometer would determine the body temperature to help approximate the time of death. A rectal thermometer was better than mottling, better than rigor, but not something to watch. The dead Susan Vandamier would then be probed, poked, and examined more thoroughly than during her last physical. And with a lot less sympathy. The final invasion and indignity would come later, during the autopsy.

Tru turned her mind back to the task at hand and walked into the room where Karen Bayborn sat quietly breathing, her grief now subdued.

"Ms. Bayborn?" Tru asked.

"Yes." The young woman turned her eyes up to Tru. She'd not moved from the spot that Tru saw her in when she had passed by the door earlier. Tru noticed a chair at a small desk near the door and pulled it over to the bedside. Before returning to Bayborn, she checked her tape recorder and loaded a fresh tape.

"Ms. Bayborn," Tru said, sitting down and looking around the room. "I have some questions I need to ask you." The decorations in the room told Tru that she was in a woman's bedroom. Pastel shades, cut flowers in a vase, billowing comforters, and piled pillows stated nesting female luxury. The closet door stood partially open, and neat rows of women's shoes peeked out to confirm her suspicions.

"I don't think I can," Karen sobbed.

"It's important, Ms. Bayborn. Very important."

Tru waited for the sobbing to subside. She had to have information now, and Karen Bayborn was the only one available to give it. Later there might be others, but Bayborn was the fish on the hook.

"Do you live here?"

"No, I — I'm a friend. I came over to visit," Karen hesitantly stated.

"You told the officer downstairs you arrived a

little after midnight. That's a little late for most social engagements," Tru prodded. She could smell the light scent of musky perfume wafting from Karen's skin. The sleek slacks and loose silk shirt accentuated the fragility of the young woman. A small gold chain fell lightly against her breasts where the collar parted to expose her cleavage. Her hair smelled freshly washed with strawberries and cream. An after-midnight social call, and she had been dressed to entice. The victim, Tru noted, had waited for a guest in her nightgown.

"She'd called earlier, I — it took me a while to come over."

"When did she call you?"

"Around eleven."

"I need you to be as precise as you can. Do you remember what time it was when she called?"

"It was eleven. Dian — Sandra woke me up. I'd been dozing; she said it was eleven. I hadn't expected her to call until later," Karen admitted.

"You started to mention someone else," Tru said as her eyes drifted back to the closets.

"Diana Merriam. Sandra's housemate and business partner. She was leaving tonight . . . a business trip or some- thing to do with her family . . . I can't remember exactly. Sandra called after she'd left."

"All right. She called you after her housemate left. It took you an hour to get here. You must live quite a distance from here?"

"Not really. I told you I'd been dozing. Actually, I fell asleep in the Jacuzzi. I cleaned up, got dressed, and drove over. We were just going to have a drink,

34

sit around, and talk. Friends do that," Karen persisted as her words spilled out defensively.

The defensiveness in the tone, the sharp crack of words, dressed to the nines, late-night rendezvous, perfume, and nightgowns caused Tru's proximity alarm to ring loudly. She stood up and looked down at Karen. Tru disliked evasiveness in witnesses and suspects. She knew enough to expect it, but she'd never liked it. The reluctance for truth always had an aggravating way of slowing her down as she searched for case solution. It raised her irritation and firmed her resolve.

"Wait here," Tru ordered and left the room.

Tru walked back into Sandra Vandamier's bedroom. She surveyed the room and, glancing around, she headed for one of the large walnut nightstands that stood silent sentry beside the bed. She pulled open the drawers and looked inside. Nothing but an assortment of late-night reading books, a pair of reading glasses, an odd piece of notepaper, and loose pens. A small, decorative metal box lay open in the bottom of the second drawer, and the torn edge of a fifty-dollar bill had lodged against the exposed latch. They weren't what she was looking for, but she made a whispered note into her tiny tape recorder to come back to it later.

Grasping the corner of the bed skirting, Tru tossed it back and found a row of drawers slightly recessed under the edge of the bed. Easily available, Tru mused to herself.

Tru put on a protective plastic glove and stirred the contents into view. There were several colorful silk scarves of varying lengths, lubricating jelly, a hand-strap vibrator, a butt plug, leather straps, various invasion devices, and a double-crowned dildo. Tru looked into the other two drawers under the bed. The restraining devices, instruments of control, subjugation, and intrusion escalated up to levels of the minor pain and torture variety. Tru stared into the drawers in perplexity and shrugged. Different people, different ways, all for different reasons. She wasn't going to judge. It wasn't her job, inclination, or avocation. It was more than she expected to find, but one item would be low key enough. She took a scarf, closed the drawer, and walked back to the room where Karen Bayborn waited.

"Shut the door," Tru directed the uniformed officer. He complied as Tru walked back to the chair, holding the scarf up to a wide-eyed Karen.

"Ms. Bayborn," Tru began slowly. "Why don't you tell me how you got inside the house, why you were coming over for a visit so very late in the evening, and why you had to wait until Ms. Vandamier's housemate left?"

"Oh, god," Karen choked.

"You can talk to me here. You can tell me about your relationship with the victim, or we'll go downtown and talk there. Your choice."

"Oh, god . . . she'll kill me . . ."

"Who will kill you? Vandamier's dead. Or is it Diana? You think she might kill you, too? Is that what worries you?"

"Diana? Diana Merriam? I don't think she'd . . ." Karen's eyes popped as she gasped at the thought. "You don't think she killed . . . oh, my god . . . she loved her."

"It would be a motive." Tru tried to hold herself firm to the line of questions. Tru's mind flitted back to the contents of the drawers. She didn't want to think about the possibilities of the devices and let her own temperament suggest to her how such things seemed to violate her sense of nonharmful relationships between women. She didn't want to know the hurt they could or needed do to themselves or to each other for gratification. She didn't want to know if it could reach the levels that men usually reserved for their treatment of women. She shook her head and realized she clung to a naive fantasy and that the use of some toys was her own issue avoidance.

"Did she know about you and Sandra?"

"I . . . what . . . ?" Karen tried to hedge.

"You and Sandra?" Tru maintained. "You have a key to the house, don't you? That's how you got in. You were expected to come up to the bedroom where Sandra would be waiting. Isn't that what usually happened? So, therefore, did Diana Merriam know about you and Sandra, the late-night visits, the business-trip trysts?" Tru said as she wound the silk scarf around her left hand and let the edges drape on either side. Karen watched Tru loop the scarf, her eyes widening in surprise. Tru meant it as an intended suggestion, a mesmerization to evoke resignation and truth from Karen.

"Miss Bayborn, I don't care what you and the deceased did together. I do care about why you are here and who committed the murder. Try to help me here."

"I don't know . . . She might have, I think so. Sandra gave me a key two months ago. She trusted me, loved me, and I loved her. Sandra told me

37

they . . . she and Diana . . . they had argued about me. Diana guessed. Sandra said she thought she'd convinced Diana that she was imagining things. She promised she'd leave her, but the time wasn't right yet," she sobbed.

Old story, Tru thought, sighing. Be with me, stay with me. I'll leave the other when the time is right. Trust me, baby, wait for me, baby, believe me, baby. Sometimes old stories worked. There was no reason to change a line when it worked most of the time, or at least worked for the one stringing along the two. Little secrets and bigger lies.

"When did Diana leave tonight?"

"I don't know. Earlier. I was so surprised when Sandra called. I thought she'd told me Diana's flight didn't leave till twelve or so. But she would have, must have, been gone by the time Sandra called."

"You let yourself in, and then what . . . ?"

"I called out to Sandra. I thought she'd be downstairs. Then I thought she was waiting up here, you know, wine, flowers. So I came up, calling her name. I almost didn't see her . . . on the other side of the bed." Karen's eyes darted at the memory of walking into the room, going into the bathroom, and then returning to the bedroom. Her eyes closed as her mind rendered the vivid images. As it played back to her, her misery choked her again.

"I started around the bed to go out to the terrace. That's when, when . . ." she whimpered.

"You touched her?"

Karen looked up at Tru in surprise. "Of course I touched her. My god, she was bleeding. I wanted her to be OK. I didn't know what to do. I tried to stop

38

the blood," she said as she looked down at her hands. "I wanted her to be alive, to be all right, to stay with me," Bayborn said as the tears streamed down her face.

"Did you see or hear anyone else in the house?" Tru began again as she walked the line between persistence and sympathy.

"No, I don't think so. I couldn't stop the bleeding. I called 911," Karen whispered, and her dazed eyes turned away from Tru.

"Then you called 911. What did you do after that?"

"I don't know . . . I just sat there, holding her hand. She got . . . she got so cold," Karen cried weakly.

Tru watched her, heard the racking, heartbroken groans gurgle up in Karen's throat. She tried to distance herself from the pain in the other woman's face. She had an objective. Training, experience, and the need for performance steeled her. Tru looked at the young woman and wondered if it was an act. Karen was a suspect. But if it was a performance, it was one of the finer acts she'd ever witnessed. Cynicism and coolness warred in Tru.

"Detective North?" Tom Garvan asked at the closed door.

Tru patted Karen Bayborn on the shoulder, stood up, and walked to the door. She opened it and saw Tom's eyes go from the bed where Karen sat and back to Tru. "Anything?" he asked.

"Probably. What do you need?"

"The photo tech has gone through the rest of the house along with the print folks. They think they've spotted some places where things are missing. Mis-arrangements, a dust circle, that sort of stuff. You want to come check it out?"

"Sure." Tru turned back to face Karen Bayborn. "Ms. Bayborn, I'm going to ask you to go with an officer downtown. I need a full report from you. Everything you saw, heard, did, and touched once you arrived here. I'll be along later." She turned to leave.

"Everything?" the word caught in Karen's throat in alarm.

"About tonight, Karen. When you got here, from the moment you arrived this evening. What you did when you walked in, where and when you found Sandra, when you made the call to 911, and what you did until the police came. If I need more than that, I'll call you or be in touch," Tru said pointedly.

Tru had almost chuckled when she realized that Karen had thought she wanted to know the details of her relationship with Sandra. The detail, the intrigue, or amorous adventure was not important unless it somehow wove itself into the case. Besides, Jones and Rhonn didn't need that sort of stimulation. She put the scarf into her jacket pocket and turned to Tom.

"We'll need to get her address and phone. Let's make sure she's the staying kind before we release her. I'd appreciate it if you would go with her to the station and make sure we get everything from her. I want a litmus test run on her and her hands checked for gunpowder. She's a suspect until we know differently. She's going to be hesitant. Sandra and she were lovers. You know as much as I do here, so keep her on the suspect list when you interview her. Get her to sign her statement, and if she confesses to anything, run with it and then get hold of me.

"About the lovers bit, I know you can handle that tactfully, because if you can't, we are very likely to lose information we need," Tru said, watching Tom out of the corner of her eyes. She had worked with him before, but lifestyles of the rich, let alone rich and lesbian, were the sort of thing that evoked inappropriate responses from most of the men and women on the force. In that regard, she didn't know what to expect from Garvan.

"Whatever floats their boat," Garvan said non-committally.

Tru turned to the uniformed officer who stood guard at the room entrance. "Keep her in there. Don't let anyone else talk to her without my OK. Detective Garvan will be back to take her downtown in a few minutes."

Without further comment, Tom Garvan guided Tru to the rooms where the technicians stood guarding their finds. The missing items seemed to be concentrated in the upper master bedroom and the office space on the first floor. A smudging of a table-top, an open drawer, and rifled desk safe stood out in clear relief. The tabletop smudge could have been the swipe of a hand as it grabbed a statue, vase, or other small object. The open drawer contained papers, a daily reminder diary, and a penknife. Tru whispered into her collar that it appeared as though someone knew where and what they were looking for.

The most troubling aspect was the desk safe. It was under a false bottom in the lower right-hand drawer. It was built in and secured with sturdy bolts disguised as drawer sliders. Its tiny door stood open, free of pry marks or gouging. Tru knew that whoever opened the safe had to have had the combination and known of its location. He or she, willingly or not, had attempted to retrieve something from its interior.

Tru glanced around the room. Except for some papers on top of the desk, everything appeared to be orderly. No struggle, no tossed furniture, no broken materials anywhere.

"Do prints. Do the whole room and windows, too," Tru directed. "There's a box upstairs in the right-hand nightstand. Dust it, too." Tru frowned at the desk.

"What are you thinking?" Tom asked, edging up beside her.

"Just that right now we've got more motives than we have bodies."

"That's not good," Tom remarked.

"No, but sometimes we don't get anything. It never rains when it can pour. Well," Tru said in exasperation, "let's get back to the nettlesome details, shall we?"

"No rest for the weary," Tom said, turning away.

"That's *wicked*, Tom. The saying goes 'no rest for the wicked.' "

"That a comment on your personal life?" Tom smiled at Tru.

"Don't you wish you knew? Now get to it and see if the boy wonder has done us any good, OK? I'll make a rough sketch of the crime scene in the bedroom, but have someone take all the exact measurements. We'll need them."

"Your wish is my heartburn," Tom chided. As he watched her figure recede down the long hallway toward the kitchen, he realized that he liked Tru. Just a little. She could raise hell, but he'd never known her to stir more than she could swim in. Rumors be damned, he thought. She was a loner, and beyond that was no skin off anyone's nose and hardly any of their business.

What Tom liked most about working with Tru was her meticulous nature. She was dependable, circumspect, decisive, and usually appropriate. He didn't care whether or not the other detectives liked her. She was methodical, asked questions, shared information, and was just caustic enough to keep the right balance of sanity while sloshing around knee-deep in muck and blood.

He'd worked with worse, far worse. He knew from experience that when it was his turn on the wheel, Tru would second him on an investigation like a champ. That was the difference between her and most of the rest of the unit. She did the job. He didn't mind her quirks or finicky, painstaking attention to details and probabilities. It was preferable to getting stuck with a rambunctious or offensive wanna-be. It was a job, and he knew they both knew how to do it.

The work required that those left at the scene slug away until the early Sunday dawn began to break faintly in the sky. Weary and worn, the techs, pathologist's crew, uniformed officers, and Tru finished the scene and trudged out into the humid morning air. The house was secured. Tru kept a key.

Tru blinked at the sky, drove her vehicle up into the driveway, and parked before the garage doors. She exited the car wearily. It felt like the beginning of a long day.

Chapter 4

Tru walked back to the end of the driveway where the perimeter line was staked out by the yellow DO NOT CROSS — POLICE LINE plastic tape. The tape snaked off across the curb for seventy feet in either direction and looped around the house. The back half of the great length of tape enclosed more of the lot at the far rear of the house and met the line of golf-course grass to finish its sloppy square. It was a flimsy barricade but enough to keep most curious citizens from risking imagined arrest or trespassing charges.

Tru looked at the four other large houses that made up the cul-de-sac. A few ancient trees had been thoughtfully left by the contractors. Where the ancient trees stopped, newer shrubbery and high privacy fences marked the perimeters of each quiet domain. No dogs had barked last night, and none were in sight this morning. The well-to-do neighborhood was quiet except for the momentary sound of a vehicle exiting a drive with children's heads jostling in the rear. The next set of houses was clumped a comfortable distance away in their own sedate cul-de-sac. The area went on that way in clusters and conclaves at ever-increasing distances from the house where murder had been committed. Peace and quiet were what the folks on south Summitt had paid for, not the intrusion of reality.

It was quiet. She could hear only the distant drone of traffic if she strained her ears. Tru smiled to herself. Privacy and an almost surreal sense of rural quiet surrounded the area. It was as close as you could get to the city and pretend to be somewhere else as you nestled among distant neighbors who cordially minded their own business. No potlucks, no yard parties or backyard cookouts ever disturbed anonymity. An assailant could have blasted away with a cannon, and people would have hesitated about going to the phone. They would have hesitated, then busied themselves with wondering if they were interfering in someone's private concern. She knew people didn't pay this kind of money in expectation of being bothered by fraternization with the community locals.

Staying on the walkway, she moved to the back of the house and noticed the lawn had been recently mowed. No flattened grass would yield a clue if the murderer's hasty retreat lay in the direction of the golf course. She tried the privacy gate and opened it to let herself in. She was surprised and wondered if an officer had unlatched it from the inside. Walking in, Tru saw lounge chairs alongside the swimming pool, found one she liked, and sat down. Shoving her sunglasses back from her face, she pulled out a fistful of Polaroids from her jacket pocket. It was time to study the scene again, while it was fresh and clear in her mind. The tranquillity of the water belied the disquiet of the death on the second floor.

Tru took out a notepad and quickly jotted down the words *murder, suicide, burglary, lover's quarrel. A or B.* Habit made her write the notes and whisper them as she wrote. Habit made sure she didn't forget even one stray thought.

There were two large categories of possibilities: the assailant who would be known by the victim, and the unknown intruder clever enough to be let in when the victim's guard was down. The unknown assailant would have been lucky to accomplish the deed and be gone between the time the housemate left and the lover arrived. The housemate could have backtracked. The young lover could have demanded an end to the charade. Leave no stone unturned, Tru chanted under her breath.

Fresh tape in the recorder, she looked at the notes and began. "*Murder*: no points of forced entry. Items taken from the upstairs room and office downstairs. Some bruising on victim's left arm and temple. Gun at point-blank range. Victim fell near phone on the nightstand. Rear door to pool area unlocked.

"*Suicide*: Victim may have been hiding or

46

destroying items from lover, either one. Point-blank range of gun, one shot to chest. Dressed for midnight dalliance. Self-recriminations for betrayal of either lover. If suicide, why wasn't she on the bed, more posed, more certain in her actions? Sloppy to stand and do it. Most women don't suicide with gun, too messy and unflattering finish. An awkward turn of the hand to get the gun to shoot direct.

"*Burglary*: House not totally ransacked, a few selected areas. Someone knew where they were going and what they were looking for. Another late-night lover? Caught her while she was back upstairs. Left the door unlocked for Karen, but Karen had a key. Gate unlocked, entry at rear of house. Carelessness allowed burglar to enter. We don't know the extent of the items taken. We don't know what things were taken. Check with insurance company and housemate for details. Lights on in house. What are chances of burglar coming in when house looked like someone awake?

"*Theft after murder*: Item taken from a tabletop. A drawer next to the bed with a metal box. Safe in desk in home office. Money, notes, papers, insurance policies, a strange assortment of possibilities. What did she have that someone else wanted? What was she hiding that someone discovered? If the burglary in safe or theft took place downstairs, why was she taken back upstairs? A botched theft culminating in an attempted rape?

"*Lover's quarrel, speculation A*: Live-in lover had not left, heard Sandra on the phone. They argued, fought, a gun, a struggle, and death. What about the look of burglary? A ruse, a way of diverting attention? When did Diana leave? Why did she leave so early? Did she come back, know what was going to happen, a confrontation out of hand? Where is Diana now?

"*Lover's quarrel, speculation B*: Karen came over, recriminations about Sandra not leaving her other lover. They argued, there was a gun, whose gun? Sandra told her to get lost. It was an ending not a continuation of their affair. They struggled and gun went off? Blood on Karen. Karen awkward in her demeanor and reluctant to admit affair, personal problems there? She would have had to ransack the areas. What would she have been looking for? She had nothing on her but could have trashed it, hidden it to pick up later. We searched her person, car, and grounds. Nothing. What was the point of the things taken? What was taken?

"Who is Karen Bayborn, who is Diana Merriam, and who was Sandra Vandamier that someone would kill her for what she had or did not have? What she would or would not do? What she was and would not change?"

Tru turned off the recorder and looked at the pictures of the victim again. The story was there in those dead eyes, but it would have to be wrested from the living. Sandra Vandamier had lied in life to her lover. Karen Bayborn, her young lover, had tried to lie to Tru. And no one had heard from the house-mate yet. Circumstances made motives out of lies. Tru wondered how many more were waiting.

Three hours later Tru had walked the circumference of the exterior of the house with her camcorder in hand and had toured the rooms of the house. She paid particular attention to the crime scene where tape delimited the area where Sandra

Vandamier was found, and to the desk safe, the smudged table, and Diana Merriam's room. She didn't forget to film any room. She did not miss or skip an area. Everything had equal importance until one or two things showed themselves as keys.

Taking another walk through the house she knew she didn't need the camera. It was a tool, a weapon to pry open the issues, a means of supplementing the imagery in her mind. It was a safety net for her compulsiveness and questioning. With the recorder she'd be able to review the entire scene as often as she needed to. She'd be able to return to the house as often as she liked until the case was solved or cold.

She didn't want it to go cold. The first eighteen to twenty-four hours of a homicide were the most important. They were vital. After that, people would make their stories, get them straight and stick to them like truth and revelation. After twenty-four hours, the things Tru and the others didn't do would haunt them like waifs vanishing in the night. Tru felt that the scene, evidence, connections, and probabilities were evaporating even as she filmed them. It was the curse of the profession, the justification for their existence, and a bit of the crucible to which they tied themselves. Diligence, luck, information, and imagination. A fairy tale for the prosaically challenged.

Chapter 5

At ten o'clock Tru returned to the office and conferred with Tom Garvan and the lab techs. Bates was sitting in his cubicle pounding out the preliminary notes that Tom and Tru handed him. He was not a happy camper, but he was the second-assist. The newest kid on the block was where the grunt work was traditionally and appropriately distributed.

"I'm going over to the pathologist's office. You want to come or stay here?" Tru asked as she passed the cubicle where Tom Garvan played hunt-and-peck on his computer keyboard. She smiled at him as she watched his fingers fly in their curious dance of single-digit duets.

"Thought you'd never ask," Garvan said, smiling up at her. He didn't care for the duty any more than Tru did.

It was required protocol to watch the autopsy. Two or three heads were always better than one.

Good pathologists, although skilled in the mysteries of mayhem, were not the detectives on the case. Not all pathologists were good. Some lacked the necessary ability for detail; some imagined themselves to be beyond reproach or questioning by investigators. Some had watched too much television. Good pathologists at autopsy recognized that they had not been to the scene and were therefore unfamiliar with some of the nuances of the offense, the available leads, and the questions or concerns of the detectives. Pathologists knew they were part of the whole process and were another turn of the wheel toward fact and case resolution. The best pathologists dared supposition and innuendo. The extraordinary never stopped learning. They were rare. A major metropolitan area was lucky to have one.

Average or excellent, all pathologists are highly skilled technicians who know anatomy, the structure of wounds, what a weapon could or could not do under given circumstances, and that they are not the beginning or end of an investigation. They are the handmaids of the tale being told by the body presented. They splay the flesh, cut the organs, photograph and note the details. They give light and form to some assumptions and facts of a case. But they can also throw question and shadow on the presumptions of the investigators. Pathologists, particularly those trained in forensics, could bring consternation to assumptions too easily offered by the investigators and the assumed muteness of death.

Dr. Camellia Houghin had been the chief forensic pathologist in Kansas City, Missouri, for more than twenty years. Lithe, wiry, quick of wit, and caustic to the timid, she was a fixture and legend in the four-state area of Missouri, Kansas, Nebraska, and Iowa. Legend said that she'd been around since Jesus was a corporal, and fact placed her in Kansas City since the Nixon administration. She was admired and respected by judges at all levels. She'd earned their respect and was a terror to the prosecution and inept investigators on either side of the question. She was respected because she was not only good at her job, she was excellent.

Dr. Houghin was sitting at her desk and smiled up at Tru when she knocked on the door. It was a large office. The oversize manager's chair all but consumed Dr. Houghin in its massiveness. A small round table used for staff conferences, case reports, and Dr. Houghin's late-afternoon teas stood to the side of the large oak desk. Books lined the tall book-cases with interesting titles like *Abnormal Homicide Investigation, Advanced Forensic Pathology*, and *Gunshot Wounds: Aspects of Firearms and Ballistics*. Light reading for insomniacs and others capable of being emotionally reserved.

"Come in, come in." Dr. Houghin waved Tru and Tom Garvan into her office. "I was wondering when you'd finally show up." She reached out and shook Tru's hand in genuine fondness. She'd known Tru since Tru joined the force. Tru had been one of the few recruits who didn't pass out, throw up, or swoon during her first autopsy. Dr. Houghin had later heard that Tru had saved her tremors until she got outside the building and into fresh air. Tru had also opted to extend her training tour for the opportunity to work alongside Dr. Houghin. Dr. Houghin had enjoyed the time with Tru during six months of forensic pathology experience and training. They had developed a sincere friendship and mutual respect for each other. Dr. Houghin had given Tru a love for the thrills of the chase in the game of murder. The experience had continued to serve Tru in the field.

"Couldn't get here any sooner," Tru said as she returned the double-clasped handshake.

"I've had the victim weighed, measured, and x-rayed by my assistants, so we don't have to waste your time with the preliminaries. We can just get right to it," Dr. Houghin said, patting Tom Garvan on the shoulder as she slid past them and out the door. At sixty she was spry and quick in body and mind. Looking at death for thirty-five years made her appreciate her own life and those she found worthy of her interest. She did what she could to combat her smoking habit and extend her time on earth. Her daily speed walk of three miles before six A.M. promoted her agility and put most of her staff to shame if they tried to keep up with her pace. As it was, Tru and Tom found themselves having a foot race with her down the hall.

The examination room area was a large twenty-five-by-seventy-five-foot room. Four stainless-steel examination tables lined up with the adjacent sinks, rolling instrument tables, and hanging scales. Air, suction, and water hoses were snapped securely to the tables in tucks and recoilers to keep them out of the way unless in use. Cold-storage chambers lined the far end of the wall, and more lay beyond the room in silent expectation.

The room was well lighted, but as she walked into the room, Dr. Houghin flipped on the bright lights above the table. Light and more light was essential for the detailed examination. Dr. Houghin reached up to turn on the microphone hanging over the table where the remains of Sandra Vandamier lay. From that point forward the subject once known as Sandra Vandamier would be referred to simply as the victim, or the body, her previous distinctiveness removed.

Clearing her throat, she began the formal litany for the recording devices. "Dr. Houghin, chief forensic pathologist for the Kansas City, Missouri, police department. License number FP 6759 through the Missouri Board of Medical and Behavioral Sciences, 1996. It is Sunday, June 16, and exactly," Dr. Houghin glanced at the clock on the wall, "eleven-seventeen A.M.

"The victim has been identified as Sandra R. Vandamier, a white female aged forty-five, and appears slightly younger than her stated age. General tonality of the skin gives appearance of healthy life habits. The body looks to be well-formed without immediately noticeable historical scars, marks, tattoos, or other surgical or cosmetic blemishes.

"A contact wound with ragged, star-shaped bursting effect due to probable contact shot is present on the breastbone. Muzzle blast has caused some tattooing around the entrance wound and is a non-perforating type.

"Victim's hands have been covered with paper bags prior to transportation to this office. Victim is clothed in a dark lavender, seemingly silk composition nightgown trimmed in a wide brocade at the neckline. There is marbling of the skin on the right side of the body from the head and down the spine area on the right side to the right and left leg, with mottling on the limbs where blood pooled in the body. A penetrating force has seemingly torn through the gown. There is charring on the fabric in the area of the sternum."

Dr. Houghin stood back from the table and looked at the body as she recited her immediate impressions into the overhead microphone. She walked from the head to the toes, traversing the area twice. Her eyes darted along the lines of the body, the exposed skin, the face, the gown, and down to the feet. She was focused and no longer aware of the visitors to her domain.

And so it began, a three-hour course of external and internal examination of the body. The gown was removed and transferred to the table where Dr. Houghin worked. It would be examined later for trace powder and pattern. She carefully washed the body, noting the size, shape, and pattern of the contact blast to the sternum as its irregular edges came into sharp relief. Other bruises and lacerations were noted.

The external examination concluded, the internal began with an examination of the head, neck, cervical spine, and downward. Dr. Houghin made note of the single trace thread from the gown that was imbedded in the chest and suspected further discoveries in the interior of the wound.

She started at the top of the head. Each area,

quadrant, and surface would be examined in its turn; an incision would be made, and examination extended into the interior until the body gave up all the facts it was hiding.

Tru fought to maintain her own focus on the examination. She was focused, but she hated it. Of all the things she could tolerate, the cranium invasion was not among them. It was the most personal, the greatest invasion, the exposing of that which had housed the seat of the personality.

Tru took it personally and had to breathe slowly through her nose to steady her wavering vision as Dr. Houghin progressed. She forced her eyes away from the face, away from what spoke of personhood, singularity, and humanness. She looked instead at the blankness and anonymity of the unoccupied form. Her mind steadied itself, and she heard the sound of Dr. Houghin's voice echoing through the buzzing rush of blood in her ears. She locked her knees and forced herself to return to the panorama of the examination. She hated it, but each time was another lesson, another set of facts, and part of the obligation she knew she owed to the victim.

Dr. Houghin completed her examinations by two-thirty. The full and final report of toxicology, spectrography, X ray, and a multiplicity of forensic details would not be available until late the following day. The reports would give minute details of the last hours of the victim's life and determine exact cause of death beyond the mere pronouncement of homicide. The reports would say how the injury insulted the body, what part compounded the other, and what system shut down first.

Tru's stomach rumbled and surged against neglect, but she refused to hear its complaints. New information had surfaced. There were bruise marks on Sandra Vandamier's wrists and upper arm and small abrasions on the skin near the right elbow. An abraded area on the left leg along the thigh with another on the kneecap suggested rug burn, as though she'd tried to rise against her assailant. At the base of her neck, scratch marks and a contusion to the back of the head were noted.

There had been a struggle. Sandra Vandamier had not gone gently into that deep night. She had fought someone, raged at their handling of her, and lost.

"I'm getting punchy," Tom Garvan complained as Tru slid into the driver's side of the unmarked car.

"Yeah," Tru agreed wearily, and grabbed the mobile phone receiver from its cradle. She punched in the numbers and waited.

"Yeah, Bob, Tru. Anything interesting from the lab or anywhere else yet?" She listened quietly as she headed back to the department. "Good. When is she coming in? Fine. OK. Then do you have any objections if Tom and I go get ourselves cleaned up?" A frown crossed her face.

"Yes, alone, to our separate homes, in our separate cars. Cripes, Bob, what's your wife been feeding you?" Tru complained into the phone as she turned her eyes in Tom's direction and rolled them skyward. "Bye."

"Don't tell me," Tom Garvan chuckled as he stared straight ahead. He didn't want to see the look in her eyes, it would only make him laugh more. He knew she wasn't prudish, but every now and again the tendency of innuendo made her bristle like a porcupine with switchblades. Exhaustion and hunger were part of the current combination of irritants.

"I won't, but I don't believe his comment has enhanced either yours or my reputation. In fact, I'm sure it didn't do mine any good." Tru shook her head.

"He only gets that way when he's tense," Garvan countered.

"Well, it's a pretty bizarre visceral response to tension. If he gets worse, I'm going to have to talk to his wife about peppering his evenings with a little more than conversation and a lot less red meat," Tru asserted. "Anyway, Chicago police have picked up Diana Merriam. She's being escorted back to K.C. International late this evening. I'll go meet her, and we should be at the office by ten-thirty. All right?"

"As good as it's going to get."

"Good. I'll drop you at your car and see you later." Tru sighed, struggling to focus on the traffic and to keep her mind's eye from reviewing the details of the case.

Chapter 6

Tru didn't go home right away. Her head was spinning, and she wanted to slow it down. She hoped the car knew the way. The sign outside was not flashing its usual strobe at three in the afternoon.

Unsuspecting sleek-suited minions of the plaza walked past the benign exterior of the Round Table. It was a women's bar for women who loved other women. It was a landmark familiar to Tru and a welcome release from the aggravations of law enforcement ever since she moved to Kansas City, Missouri, twenty years ago. Few, if any of the regulars would be gathered inside at this hour on a Sunday. It could stay open on Sundays because they served food. The Round Table had the best pizza within a five-mile radius, and customers were extremely loyal.

Tru steered the car into the parking lot next door and secured her sunglasses to protect her eyes from the wave of heat and glare bouncing off the white tiles of the buildings along the opposite side of the street. As staggering as the heat, the blast of cold air from the interior of the bar drew the skin on her arms up like a pucker. The high, bright sun vanished from view and memory four feet inside the door.

She blinked, squeezed her eyes tight, and opened them again. A few dark images seemed to dash out of the dark and settle into a semblance of bar, tables, and pool players on the edge of her vision. Tru and Eleanor had occasionally frequented the bar. They'd even danced a few times.

Eleanor, Tru thought ruefully. Eleanor and she had been lovers for a little less than three years. Each year had seemed longer, less happy, and more confining for Tru. The more Tru flinched away from the criticisms, the more Eleanor had become repressive, controlling, and unkind. But it had been Eleanor who had finally left Tru. Left her for another woman and left Tru staggering under the weight of the loss.

It was to the Round Table that Tru had returned several weeks after Eleanor left. Tru had spent a chilled night in March watching the trains pull out of Kansas City from her perch high on the bridge. She'd met Marki in the Round Table bar on the night that Tru had wondered about the futility of feeling.

A smile came to Tru's lips as she remembered.

She had been drinking fairly heavily, drowning between regret and relief from Eleanor. Marki later had to tell Tru some of what they had done that night, what Marki did to her under the bar while the strobe lights flashed and played. She didn't have to be told what Marki could do to her or what she could do for Marki anymore. Tru had sobered up, gotten her life on track, and begun learning to care again because of Marki.

"Come here right after church did you?" a voice cut easily through the dark at her.

"I hit high mass late most times," Tru bantered back at Victoria, or Vic to long-time acquaintances.

Vic, a former cross-country, long-distance runner, walked over to the end of the bar and waited for Tru to sit. Vic hadn't been in a marathon in three years. An automobile accident had taken away her long-term ambitions and rearranged them into a more restricted life. She'd been lucky, or at least as lucky as bad luck could get. The bigger, heavier car had turned into her. Its front fender and tire sliced through the soft pliable metal of Vic's aging Geo like a hot knife through butter. The tiny car was jammed down the street for twenty feet until it slammed up against a telephone pole. The double impact broke Vic's femur, and the tire rested on her for over an hour while firefighters and paramedics attempted to extract her from the wreckage.

"Like hell. Last time you saw the inside of a church, I heard tell some stained glass broke." The limp was less exaggerated after three operations and years of therapy.

"Might have, but only a hair's breadth and that for anticipation," Tru said as she glided onto a stool.

"Want the usual?"

"No. I need to be able to drive home. Haven't eaten all day. By the way, it is still Sunday, isn't it?" Tru mused as she pointed to the draft spigot for a draw. A short beer or two and then home, she advised herself.

"Was when I got here. What have you been up to?" Vic asked quizzically. She wiped the already clean spot in front of Tru with the bar rag, placed a coaster in front of her, and set down the short beer.

"Working. Better give me a glass of water, too," Tru said as she tipped the beer back and felt the cold slide down her throat.

"That's a hell of a thing to do on a perfectly nice weekend." Vic smiled at her, nodded, and walked to the other end of the bar where another hot and thirsty customer had landed.

The beer went down like water, and Tru waved to Vic. The second went down only a little slower as Tru spaced it with the real water to keep the alcohol content from hammering her to the bar stool. It almost worked. But the combination of heat, beer, sleep loss, and lack of food made her eyes feel like they were beginning to waver in her head. She looked at the pizza menu tacked to the mirror behind the bar and speculated about food. Indecision overwhelmed her until a voice whispered suggestively behind her back.

"Now, if you're looking for something good, I have what you need." Marki's voice flowed over her like a healing.

"You know what kind of people hang out in places like this, don't you?" Tru teased, and turned to kiss

Marki. The bar had been her hope for refreshment, but Marki was the oasis to her thirst.

"I've heard stories. Why else do you think I'm here?"

"Could be they were just stories? Could be you've been misinformed? Could be you have an overactive imagination?"

"Could be," Marki said as she put both arms around Tru. "Could be it's time for you to come home? I've been calling you all day. I finally gave up and called the station. They said you'd been tied up since early morning but called out to go home a little bit ago."

"I was on my way," Tru explained as Marki hugged her and let go to take a stool next to her. "How did you know to come here?"

"Easy. I've been hanging around this cop lately. I've learned one thing . . ." Marki smiled and leaned forward to kiss Tru. It was a soft, soul-rocking kiss.

". . . and what might that be?" Tru asked, trying to steady herself against the draw of the kiss.

"Just that when it has been a little too ugly, a little too bothersome, you stop here for a quick one. I'll assume that it's only been a beer. It's not like it ever works, you know," Marki told her frankly.

"Not like what doesn't work?"

"It doesn't work. Having a drink after you've seen more human heinousness in one day than anyone should in a lifetime. It doesn't take it from your eyes." She kissed Tru on each of her eyes. "Doesn't take it from your forehead." She kissed the furrows that had worked their way across Tru's brow. "And it doesn't take it from that petulant set of your lips,"

Marki said as she kissed the corners of Tru's mouth and then kissed her again full on the lips. Her tongue darted and teased at Tru's teeth.

"What does work?" Tru found her voice faint and reluctant after the branding Marki's had left.

"Well, I was wondering when you might ask that very question," Marki said as she took Tru's hand and drew her off the bar stool. "Why don't you come home to my house and we'll try to figure that one out."

Tru tossed a dollar on the counter as a tip and waved back at Vic as she was led from the bar.

"You kids play nice now," Vic said cheerfully at their retreat.

Tru left the unmarked unit in the parking lot. She didn't want to risk the drive across town to the slight buzz the beers had produced in her brain. It wouldn't have served Tru to be in a fender bender with the smell of alcohol on her breath. Marki drove them to the door of her house and into the garage. They'd ridden in pleasurable silence, fondly touching hands and cheeks the short distance to Marki's house.

Marki lived close to the University of Missouri at Kansas City where she was the chair of the psychology department. She'd bought the house shortly after her arrival to take up her post two years ago. It was a two-story brick, built in 1908 of heavy timber and native stone, with a basement on the sturdy bedrock of limestone that ran through the rolling bluffs. It had been remodeled by a minister and his wife during their tenure in the seventies and eighties at a nearby Lutheran church. They had returned the pocket doors to their setting, removed the awful paint that had covered the hardwood trim and banisters, and steamed off the garish coverings of wallpaper faded by the light of multiple bay windows staggered throughout the house. The fireplace had been restored to use and provided an attractive central feature between the drawing room and living room areas.

Tru followed Marki through the breezeway, past the enclosed garden shelter of the Jacuzzi, and into the kitchen.

"Go on into the living room," Marki said. "I'll be with you in a moment." As Tru settled into the living room, Marki brought out a tray of cheese, summer sausage, delicately sliced dill pickles, and crackers. She turned and went over to the wet bar, but not before she winked lovingly at Tru. The plate of treats she'd prepared for Tru was enough to give Marki heartburn, but Tru enjoyed the combinations. Marki obligingly indulged Tru, even if it meant having to watch her eat something as cholesterol laden as sausage. She knew Tru didn't have too many vices, and the ones she did have were the type of immoderations they both enjoyed.

"I can't stay long," Tru announced as Marki returned from the wet bar near the fireplace with a beer for Tru and a glass of wine for herself.

"Oh, why's that?" Marki narrowed her eyes in mock suspicion. "And what's her name?"

"Actually," Tru smiled coyly at Marki, "there are two of them. One's name is Sandra Vandamier, but she's not going anyplace, and the other is Diana Merriam. I'm picking her up at the airport at ten-thirty this evening." Tru laid the information teasingly at Marki's feet in anticipation of a squall.

There was no harm meant. It was a rib, and further provocation meant to put Tru on the upside of the needling.

"Sandra Vandamier? You can't be serious. That woman's nothing but trouble, and I've never heard of anyone getting out of her lair unscathed!" The look on Marki's face was compelling and filled with disapproval. She'd been dating, courting, and engaged in mutual seduction with Tru for over three months. She wondered how many more sides to Tru there might be if this were the revelation of interests that she thought it might be.

"No, seriously. But Sandra Vandamier isn't going to be doing anyone harm or mischief again. Not in this life. And if the wheel turns the way it should, not the next either. Someone killed her this morning. The odds-on favorite at this point is the other woman I mentioned, Diana Merriam," Tru confessed.

"Sweet goddess," Marki breathed. "Is that why I couldn't find you today? Is that where you've been? Poor thing," Marki said as she swept down on the couch to sit next to Tru. She knew how Tru abhorred the sight of pain and suffering. On a number of occasions Marki had asked Tru why she stayed in law enforcement when the daily cruelties people inflicted on each other bothered her.

The dark looks she'd received from Tru in return for the questions had limited Marki to three attempts to unravel that small mystery by probing. She had promised Tru that she would refrain, as much as possible, from playing psychologist with her. She didn't want Tru as a client. She wanted her as she was, her lover. Tru was something of an enigma and the most interesting lover Marki had known in years.

If someone unraveled Tru too soon or slipped in the dissection, they might unravel the wrong thread, only to be lost and misled. Worse, Tru would most likely vanish from her life without a backward glance. The issue of law enforcement was closed for the time being, and Marki knew it would remain that way until Tru chose to tell Marki on her own. Marki knew that Tru would have to come to trust her more, and that meant time.

"Another day, another fifty cents," Tru chimed in mock derision.

Marki set her drink on the table and took Tru's from her hand. "Come here," Marki encouraged as she wrapped her arms around Tru.

Tru leaned into Marki's arms and was rocked in the soft, gentle sway of her lover's caress. Marki's hand stroked Tru's forehead, rubbing the temples and massaging upward to the crown of her head. She felt Tru's shoulders relax and the tenseness in her back begin to uncoil. She touched Tru's face and let her fingers glide down to the first button on Tru's blouse to release it from its fastening. Marki heard a humming sigh free itself from Tru's throat as Tru turned in expectation into Marki's arms.

Their lips pressed softly together in sweet straining as they reclined further on the couch. Tru's hands reached up to cradle Marki's face as she moved against her and deeper into the kiss.

Marki turned, her longer frame taking Tru with her as she rolled to leave them lying side by side. Tru groaned as Marki pressed her thigh between her legs, forcing them apart. The responsiveness and need she felt returning through Tru's body heightened Marki's own desire. Marki rocked her leg forward and pulled Tru down the chino fabric to ride its taunting length. Spreading her hands over Tru's muscled buttocks, she stretched her long fingers around the straining haunches and was rewarded with the unabashed press of the fiery arousal she'd ignited in Tru.

Holding onto her with one hand, Marki quickly slipped the other between the contact of their bodies and found the button and zipper of Tru's pants to release them. As she slipped her hand past the unlocked barriers, Marki thrust her fingers forward and clasped the slick silk beneath.

Tru's mouth sought hers in grinding necessity. Marki returned the kiss, touching Tru's lips with hers, sliding them along, making Tru strain to capture the elusive delight. She licked Tru's lips and pressed urgently into the succulent mouth, teaching Tru the truth about one need calling to another, one wetness pursuing another, and one desire obtaining its delight. Tru was an apt and eager student, and Marki was mentor to Tru's yearnings.

Marki's fingers teased the slickness. Tru arched and thrust against Marki's probing fingers, her mouth opening in startled surprise as surely as her soft wetness opened to Marki's insistence. Marki pushed down on Tru's hips with her body as she thrust her hand up against the straining material. In one swift flick of her fingers Marki pulled the encumbering elastic leg of Tru's panties away from what she sought. As she slid two fingers into the deepness she lingered against the erect clitoral nipple of Tru's craving.

"I . . . want . . . to . . . do .|. . you," Tru's breath punctuated the words into Marki's mouth. "It's not fair, you always get me so hot," she gasped. "So easy, so easy for you." Her voice came in staccato whispers.

"Ohhnnn," Tru pleaded, and rode the thrust of her lover to the crescendo that awaited. Marki could feel her tense. The muscles her fingers touched punched, strained, and grasped at her hand. Marki rode the wave with Tru. Up and onward until it didn't seem possible that it would ever end. Then it came. Tru's electrifying orgasm rocked Marki in delight and wonder. It rocked her in amazement and the incredible ecstasy of shared pleasure. She'd known women whose bodies seemed to sear in climax, but Tru was the first woman she'd ever met whose very soul seemed to simultaneously palpitate. Tru seemed so spellbound at her touch, and was so completely transported each and every time, it was the most astonishing thing Marki had ever known.

It was thrilling, compelling, and commanding of her full attention as she neared her own unfettered peak. Tru rocked and bucked under her, rubbing her leg across Marki's alert and tender crotch. Marki felt her passion swell to overflowing with the profound consummation that comes from thoroughly captivating and transporting the person you love. Marki rode the wave of unbridled triumph and rode it with Tru.

Stretched to the limit and a little beyond to the accompanying delight of future tantalization, Tru collapsed into Marki's comforting arms feeling spent and outmaneuvered.

"Not fair," Tru asserted as she snuggled closer into Marki's arms.

"I promised to be a lot of things to you, for you, and with you," Marki reminded her. "But I never said I defined playing fair by letting or requiring you to be second to my first. I don't demand that you be a miniature macho after five, or any other form of your previously well-guarded subterfuge."

"Subterfuge?" Tru said exhaustedly as she tried to rouse herself. She felt spent physically and emotionally. Her eyelids fluttered and tried to close.

Softly, Marki whispered in Tru's ear. "Subterfuge, false representation, a craftily constructed artifice of self-protection. The stuff you try so hard to wrap yourself in. To hide, not out of deceit, but for some reason you won't yet share. It's all right. I don't intend to harm you. I simply . . ." and Marki wondered how simple it might actually be. Wondered at what balance or shape their lives together would take.

"I see you. I see into you, not through you, but to the you that you try so hard to hide," Marki said, kissing her lightly on her forehead. She held Tru and listened as her breathing became deeper, signaling sleep, comfort, and genuine rest.

Later, Marki disengaged herself without disturbing Tru's slumber. She sat in a chair watching, wondering about the mettle they'd have to find and share to make an enduring permanence of their relationship possible. It could be worth it, but Tru would sooner or late have to find a way to meet her halfway. She didn't want to change or rearrange Tru, but she did want the genuine article.

"Time and patience," Marki thought. She remembered how they'd met, how she had seduced Tru when Tru had been at a very low rebound point. She wondered if she had taken advantage of Tru, used her innate sensuousness against her and used the tricks of the psychological trade to keep her.

Marki watched Tru sleeping on the couch. As much as Tru was open to her, she remained a closed book. She'd partially shared the story of her abandoning lover, Eleanor, but had not been inclined to talk in detail about her life before that time. Tru would also share with Marki some of the highlights and intrigues of an investigation if it was interesting or perplexing. But the thing that gnawed at Marki was that Tru always spoke in terms of *thinking* about a thing rather than her *feelings* about a thing. Anything.

When Marki asked Tru how she felt about their developing relationship, how she felt about being together and becoming a couple, Tru would become a little evasive. She responded to Marki's gentle and surreptitious inquiries by using think-word terms and omitting or forgetting the feel-word terms. Tru used words like *thought, reason, contemplate*, and *evaluate*. Never *feel, touch*, or *sense*. Marki hoped it was just another way of translating the world, not a deficiency. Time and patience, Marki prayed. Time and patience might win the answers and the way to Tru's heart. Marki also prayed that she had enough time with Tru to help heal the hurts that seemed so close to Tru's emotional surface, and enough patience to see it through.

At nine o'clock in the evening as the twilight settled darkly on the land, Marki gently nudged Tru to coax her awake.

71

"You need to wake up now," Marki urged reluctantly. She couldn't imagine that four hours of sleep would give Tru the rest she needed. But she didn't want her to miss her appointed round at the airport. It was harder to wake her than to let her sleep. But Tru had somewhere else to go, and her job wasn't over for the day.

"Harrumph," Tru managed.

It made Marki smile. The unintelligible words from that sleep-tangled mouth appealed to her.

"Really," Marki insisted. "Time to get up and get going."

"OK. I'm awake," Tru said as she stretched and yawned.

"It's nine. You have enough time to eat a bite and shower. Or, shower and eat a bite, depending on your inclination."

"Coffee?" Tru asked hopefully.

"What do I get in return?"

"My undying devotion?" Tru suggested, a smile passing over her lips. She loved looking, touching, and being with Marki. Over the last three months Tru had felt confused as she simultaneously wanted to pull Marki closer into her life and hold her away.

"You have some of that to give?" Marki questioned earnestly. She wasn't playing anymore. She'd been struggling with the weight of her feelings over the last three months. She didn't want to press, but at that moment she did not know how not to.

Startled by the sound in Marki's voice, Tru roused herself to full attentiveness and assessed the tone she'd heard. She considered Marki's words, her own flirtatious remark, and the questioning with which Marki had engaged her.

"Excuse me?" Tru struggled. She didn't want a rending of feelings. She didn't want to struggle against what she felt. But she didn't know how to answer Marki.

"What did you say you would give for a cup of coffee?" Marki lied through her teeth, choosing to change the tone and direction of the question. This woman possessed her, as surely as she could possess this woman physically. She, this other, possessed more of her than Marki cared to admit to herself.

The silence was deafening. They looked at each other in their segregated confusion and need.

Damn, Marki cursed, pleaded, and let the anger abate in her heart. Did Tru have no idea, was there no way of getting to her through the shield she wore against her breast? Against her heart? What wrong had been perpetrated to make Tru's heart reluctant to accept loving penetration? Is she a lock? Am I a key? Marki wondered in her silent exasperation.

Tru worried at Marki's perplexed brow. What did I do, what should I do, how can I help us? Tru tore at herself in misery. I want you, she yearned, at Marki. But you've been here before, her mind tautly reminded her. This is different. No it's not. It could be! The words fought in her head.

"I have to go," Tru said, trying to reject the confrontation. She had no wish to hurt Marki or to begin an expedition neither of them wanted to take. She rose to go to the bathroom, but her mind flashed on the tenderness of the afternoon and her knees buckled under her. Marki's back was turned to Tru as she tended to the preparations of a meal. Tru looked at her. She saw Marki's back, shoulders, and arms moving in the deliberate ballet of food preparation. Tru weakened. Her feelings were close to the surface, and her tears worked their way out of her eyes to hotly caress her cheeks.

What could she tell Marki? What would make sense in a senseless situation? She loved Marki, but she would rather lose her than have her cursed with the wheel Tru had been given to ride. Love is letting go, Tru wept to herself. Love is letting go of someone as vibrant, real, and caring as Marki. Marki was, Tru realized, the last great joy she might know. She wanted her safe, secure, and happy, deliriously so. Marki's joy was all Tru wanted, and everything she needed.

Chapter 7

Tru stood at gate C-15 waiting for the passengers to deplane. A dark blue, double-breasted blazer, a white shirt open two buttons from the collar, creased tan slacks, and her black flat dress shoes made her stand out from the blue jeans and sweats worn by the other people milling about.

The terminal was an odd mix of gray-slate concrete buttresses, walls, and ceilings with a striped parquet wood floor. It was a wide, curving half-moon design dotted with newspaper stands, baggage carousels, ticket counters, and miniature bars.

Security cameras were hidden in the concrete arches. Fluorescent lights were buried in the ceiling and glared down on hapless transits. Security officers, ticket handlers, and weary waiters dotted the hollow interior like misplaced toys.

Tru waited for two particular passengers. One would be a bleary-eyed detective from Chicago performing his or her escort duty of an equally bleary-eyed Diana Merriam. Tru had asked the Chicago police department not to question her suspect in any manner. But she knew the drill. Detectives, like buzzards, like to circle a possible kill. Only first-rate detectives could keep the questions from coming to their lips, from prying when it wasn't their concern. Nature might hate a vacuum, but detectives hated unsolved riddles with greater fervor.

Chicago had informed Tru that Diana Merriam's story about visiting an aging aunt in the hospital had checked out. The elderly Merriam had been hospitalized after a fall in her home resulted in a broken hip. Diana Merriam was the only living relative of the maiden aunt. But that instance might have been a happy coincidence for the potential felon. Real truth was yet to be discovered. The flight had been delayed by a thunderstorm over Saint Louis.

Tru tried to practice patience as she used the half-circle arching of the terminal layout as her personal speed-walking track. There were few visitors, well wishers, and late travelers to notice her race against boredom. She wanted to think about how to proceed with the interviewing of Diana Merriam, and the walking helped. There were tricks of the trade in investigation, techniques and strategies to wring truth from even the most reluctant. Tru knew she would have to get the full measure of Diana Merriam before choosing the procedures that would garner the best results.

The airline announced the late arrival, and Tru took up her post. She stood to the side of the gate exit with her badge case flipped open in her jacket pocket, the gold glint signaling the Chicago escort. Then she saw them. A frumpy, disheveled young man loped behind a stately, well-dressed woman who looked ready for the dance.

Tru watched without signaling as the woman cast her eyes over the crowd at the exit. Diana Merriam was poised and alert. She did not give the appearance of rumpled exhaustion that Tru had half anticipated. This was a woman who knew who she was, where she was. She exhibited animation and focused orientation to her surroundings. She did not display anxiety, dread, or trepidation. Tru anticipated a challenging interview.

Without blinking, the woman looked at Tru and the gold shield winking on her jacket and walked directly toward her. An amused grin crossed Diana Merriam's face as she extended her hand to Tru. Tru smiled inwardly as she saw the recognition on Diana Merriam's face and remembered her own proximity alarms.

"Detective North," Diana Merriam's voice pleasantly breathed, "how nice to meet you." Diana's short blond hair bounced in rich, thick abundance to the nape of her neck. Her pink, multiseason wool suit was complemented by a cream-colored shell and set off by delicate gold chains cascading to the shapely roundness of her breasts. Deep blue eyes twinkled down from her five-foot-eight height into Tru's gaze.

"It's a pleasure to meet you." Tru smiled lightly back.

"Will we be going straightway to your office?" Diana Merriam asked.

"Yes. Do you have bags?" Tru said, turning up the volume on a formal approach to the winsome blond standing before her. Diana Merriam oozed good manners and an easy, engaging grace. Tru imagined the young detective had been no match for Diana.

"Yes. Harley, could you get my bags for me?" Diana Merriam turned slightly to the young detective standing behind her. An embarrassed grin flickered across his face, and he obediently jogged off toward the baggage carousel.

Diana turned her attention back to Tru with a mockish grin. "He's been a very nice boy."

"I'm sure he has," Tru said, barely able to keep the grin from her face. She knew it was more than a sure bet that the nice-boy detective had not pried into Tru's investigation. But she wondered if she should call Chicago P.D. and ask them if Harley's mother knew where he was.

Tru dismissed Harley of Chicago when he returned with Diana's bags. He told her he intended to visit cousins in the Raytown area. Tru wished him a safe journey and escorted Diana Merriam to the unmarked car.

As Diana Merriam settled into the front passenger seat, Tru punched the ON button of the tape recorder in her jacket pocket. They rode silently together as

Tru turned the car onto Interstate 29 South and back into the glow of the city.

"How long will this take, Detective?"

"First," Tru began, "do you understand that you are not under arrest at this time? And that you do not have to answer any questions?"

"Yes."

"Good. Then it will take as long as you wish to discuss the events of the situation." The tape would record the contents of their chat for half an hour, all perfectly legal.

" 'The events of the situation.' What a nice, noninjurious way of phrasing a murder. Do they train you that way, or are you always so gentle with suspects?" Diana asked, turning in the seat to look carefully at Tru.

"Training," Tru said, momentarily returning Diana's stare. "If it was not for the academy, I'd still be just plain rude to everyone I met," Tru rebutted, using the tonal qualities of a rube.

"How very assertive and butch of you, Detective North."

"Miss Merriam, we have a great deal to talk about, and all of it serious. Perhaps you should carefully consider the situation. My assertiveness can override my otherwise pleasant manners, I assure you."

"No need to, Detective. You exude an appropriate professional demeanor and confidence. I'd be pleased to continue our conversation. What did you wish to know?"

"I understand you were housemates with Sandra Vandamier? Why don't you tell me about that?" Tru waited in silence as Diana considered the question. She waited for the lies, the little ones and big ones. The web of ill-conceived conspiracy most people unwittingly pulled about themselves when confronted or pushed. Little lies, buried truths, subterfuge, and deceits were the province of investigations. Half-truths emerged, sometimes bobbing to the surface like slowly drowning swimmers. Just enough truth to help the lies slide down the uncritical, untested, and uncynical mind. Tru was not troubled by a lack of training on cynicism.

"We were housemates, as you put it, for five years. I knew Sandra a little over eight years. In fact, it was eight years ago last April when she bought controlling interest in my restaurant. The other controlling, or should I say compelling, interest came later. So, you see, we were business partners first."

"Then she didn't actually own the restaurant?"

"No. She owned most of it. Sixty percent. Enough to give her the ability to make all of the decisions: hiring, firing, menu, advertisements. And the ability to scrape the lioness's share from the profits."

"Why did you sell her controlling interest?"

"I had to. It's as simple as that. As simple as an act of desperation. My father owned the restaurant originally. He died ten years ago. My mother died long before that. I was twenty-six, frivolous, living on my trust fund, and a professional student majoring in personal and a few academic whims. When my father died, Phoebe's Phoenix became my whim. I almost whimmed it right into bankruptcy. Diana saved me, my livelihood, my inheritance, and the restaurant."

"How did you meet her? How did she come to

make the offer of saving you from your problems?" Tru carefully skirted any remark, question, or inquiry regarding the murder. She had to be sure not to let any of the questions focus on Diana Merriam as the central suspect. If Diana Merriam strayed, or if Tru's questions became too pointed, it would be time for the Miranda warning. And Tru did not want that to happen until she got Diana Merriam into the interview room at police headquarters.

"She wandered into the restaurant one day. Even as a poorly suited owner/manager, I still worked every day at that time. She just wandered in like any other customer, but she kept coming back. Sandra was there every day for dinner.

"I can tell you, Detective, that constancy in and of itself was unusual. I mean, the meals were decent back then, but not the sort of fine cuisine, delicate flavors, and eye-pleasing culinary celebrations they've been these last six years. Sandra did that. She had a knack for it. She had a knack for a lot of things." Diana smiled weakly at Tru as she clasped and unclasped her hands on her lap.

"How did you feel about her taking over what had been yours?" Tru glanced sideways at Diana. A smirk danced briefly and singularly on the left side of Diana's face.

"Why, Detective North, I loved her and hated her simultaneously, of course. But then, she had that effect on people."

Tru waited in unresponsive silence.

"Have you ever loved something or someone who wasn't healthy for you, Detective North?" Diana Merriam began. "Have you ever craved the worst thing or the best thing because you needed it, had to have it, even if it meant losing yourself to it? Have you ever abandoned yourself to a need so consuming, so humiliatingly overpowering and wonderful that nothing else in the world could live in that rarefied air?" Diana stopped as she choked back a softly-breaking sob.

"No," Tru said, whisperingly low.

"Then . . ." Diana coughed and tugged ineffectually at the skirt of her dress. "Then . . . I don't know whether to congratulate you or pity you," she said flatly.

"Hated and loved her simultaneously?" Tru encouraged. "If she were such an entrepreneurial wizard and if she saved you from financial ruin as you claim, what was there to hate?"

"Are you being coy, Detective?" Diana Merriam's voice shifted to sarcastic.

"Coy, as in elusive?"

"That badge isn't big enough for you to hide from those who have eyes, Ms. Detective North, but we'll play it your way," Diana said, inhaling deeply. "My housemate, as you so decorously put it, was one of the most accomplished seductresses it has ever been my delight and disquiet to meet. But the distinction of falling under her spell wasn't mine alone. Sandra had the facility, the empathic gift, and the psychologically-twisted vitality to fathom all the emotional, sexual, and libidinous needs of anyone, any woman, she set her mind on. And, from those cognitive fathoms, she could prime, plumb, and pump you until she had you spilling out like a fountain. I craved it. Craved it with her. She could get me to do and want to do anything for her.

"Once I fucked, and got fucked with and by, two

other entrancing women while she watched. I did it, allowed it, and reveled in it based on her promise that she'd make love to me again. I let the others move against me, rub their breasts over me like so much fine heat, tongue my nipples, my ass, and my cunt. While they worked me over from every possible angle, they exposed me to Sandra in a hundred sweet, cringing, submissive contortions, while she sat there and applauded their efforts. Every swoon, pleading, and ache that trembled through their bodies was redoubled and echoed in mine. I was lost and awash in a sea of hot, pounding woman-flesh, slick, scented cunts, slavish tongues, and slippery need.

"And I loved it. I hated her for it, and loved the promise of her. That's what she could do, did to me, did to make me love her and hate her in the same costly breath. Is that illustrative and helpful enough, Detective?"

"Completely," Tru said, thankful for the night that hid the blush on her face from Diana Merriam. Tru had listened to the frank, explicit discussion, heard it all but also felt that not all was said.

Chapter 8

Tru drove into the underground garage at the police station. The tape recorder was full. Amusement spread across her face as she wondered what the transcribing pool would do with the tape. It was sure to set up a lively conversation among the ladies in the pool.

Once inside the office, Diana consented to let Tru photograph and fingerprint her for comparison use. Diana had chuckled and told Tru that as Sandra's housemate she stood a very good chance of having her fingerprints all over the house, and that the routine seemed fruitless. Tru ignored her flippant remark except to thank her for her cooperation.

Tru escorted Diana Merriam through the office and into the waiting interview room. Diana had declined coffee and was left to her own thoughts while Tru went to find Tom Garvan.

Twenty minutes later Tru and Garvan were standing on the other side of the two-way mirror looking at Diana Merriam sitting in the interview room.

"What do you think?" Garvan asked.

"She talks a lot, but not a thing about the murder. Yet. Nothing about the way Sandra's death has affected her, no remorse, tears, or questions about Sandra's death. It makes me more than a little curious and interested in her as the prime suspect. Additionally, she's not fidgeting or sleepy. Not a good sign. What have you got for me?"

"No record. She's clean as a whistle. I don't think she's ever gotten a parking ticket. Insurance and a will Merriam's attorney drew up a couple of months ago says she gets it all if anything happened to Sandra Vandamier. No huge debts, hers or Vandamier's, so there were no money problems. She's a straight-arrow there. The serial number of the gun showed it as having been purchased by Vandamier six months ago. I wonder what she was nervous about? And the lab says that Vandamier's prints were on the weapon but there were other prints as well.

"Several employees told Bates that Sandra and Ms. Merriam had a nasty lover's argument in the office a few days ago. Apparently, Ms. Merriam had a thing for Sandra, and Sandra was screwing around on her. Makes your stomach kinda turn a little, doesn't it?" Garvan nudged Tru conspritorily and waited for agreement. None came. "Are you the good cop or am I?" Garvan coughed and smiled, trying to recover.

"Take her prints down to the lab and have one of the guys do a quick check. I'm going to need all the tools I can get to use on Ms. Merriam in there. Even if there are no matches, run it in to me and I'll use it as a ruse."

"Fine. So, you're the bad cop, then?" Garvan tried again to get Tru to ease up on her intensity. It was that intensity that Garvan knew unnerved the other detectives.

"I'm good. But we do this subtly or this little socialite will be screaming for her attorney before we know it. I listened to her go on all the way back from the airport. She's a no-holds-barred woman. She had more than enough motive, time to do the deed, then get out of Dodge and provide herself with a slick little alibi. She's a critical thinker, but she likes to shock. Let's see if she'll shock me by confessing. Done right, and if I get lucky, we could have the truth before morning."

Garvan waited behind the mirror for his cue. Tru entered the interview room and laid a piece of paper in front of Diana Merriam.

"Diana Merriam, that is a copy of the Miranda warning and your rights. Let's read it together, and at each line I want you to initial it to show that you have in fact read and understood what it says." Tru read the rights and watched Diana Merriam dutifully initial each area and sign at the bottom of the form.

"You should know that it is our policy to tape all interviews. If you look at that glass partition," Tru said, pointing to the wall, "that's where the camera is. We do this so that later if your attorney claims that we hurt you, threatened you, or in any way intimidated you with anything other than the facts, we can successfully refute your claim," Tru said as she did her look-busy shuffle of the papers in front of her.

"I see," Diana commented unaffectedly, and handed the signed form to Tru.

"Why don't you begin by telling me what you know about Sandra Vandamier," Tru suggested.

Diana looked at the mirror and back at Tru. She coughed lightly and smiled into the mirror. She winked slyly at Tru and relaxed into the hard wooden chair. Her posture was confident and poised, and it radiated rehearsal.

"I knew Sandra for eight years. She said she'd been living in Kansas City about two months before I met her. There was something about inheriting a small fortune and how she'd moved to Kansas City, Missouri, to get free of small-town minds. She never talked about her family, what she did before she moved here, childhood sweethearts, or anything else. But that sort of mundane chattering would have been the least interesting or intriguing aspects of her personality. The money, sensuality, and mystery, as though she'd been dropped off by a passing UFO, was part of her charisma and charm. That and she was beautiful and had, what shall we say, exotic sexual interests, of course.

"When I first knew her, it was flattering to be with her, to be desired by her. She had money and spent it freely, taking me to the opera, ballet, and concerts. You see, I'd been struggling so long with the restaurant, and she arrived like a godsend. She didn't do many drugs and drank only occasionally. That was refreshing. The only pillow talk she was interested in was what I had to say about the business and what I wanted her to do to me.

"It was what the old Harlequin romances would call a whirlwind courtship. One day I was a nearly bankrupt owner of a sinking business. A few months later, I was a partner with a woman who could and would run my club like she ran the bedroom. She was a dynamo. Cold as ice when she wanted to be, hot as lava the next moment, and smooth as silk if she wanted something from you. But . . ." Diana Merriam faltered. She knotted her fingers and slumped visibly in the chair.

"But?" Tru suggested.

"But, it seems as though she went out of my life like she came in, feetfirst and still smoldering in mystery. I just, I realized just this minute how much I didn't know her. We were so close, so much of each other, or at least I was so fixated on her . . . but I didn't know her, really. Other than being my sweet domineering keeper for years, I have no idea who or what she was, except desirable." Diana Merriam stared wonderingly at her hands as though she might find the answer in them.

"You mean to tell me that a woman waltzes into your restaurant, picks you up, you don't know her from Eve and you nonchalantly turn your life over to her?"

"That's right, Detective. She was that sort of woman. I thought about leaving her. Thought about it again when I was sitting with my aunt in the hospital in Chicago. I might have this time, but I don't have to now, do I? May I smoke in here?" Diana asked Tru. Tru didn't respond immediately. As Diana raised her eyes from her hands, Tru saw the other woman bite her lower lip trying to keep something inside.

"Go ahead," Tru said. Watching other people smoke always made her want a cigarette, but she'd finished her last one several hours ago and, according to her discipline, wasn't due for another until seven in the morning. The clock on the wall ticked slowly toward midnight.

"You speak very fondly of her but don't seem terribly upset that she's dead," Tru whispered.

"I'm almost surprised it didn't happen sooner. She was as easy to hate as she was to love and be loved by. You could get skin close to her but not a breath closer. She didn't trust or really care for anyone else but herself. I'd wished her dead a hundred times, but it would have been like telling her no. And I never said no to anything she wanted."

"How's that again?"

"Look, she was a player. She used people, and sometimes she used them until there was nothing left. She liked to have control. She liked being in charge. She liked to see people beg for what they needed from her. Staff, lovers, associates, and me. Staff had their jobs, careers, or families to support. Other restaurateurs had their businesses to run, but she could get to some of them, too. Lovers. She surrounded herself with a smorgasbord of opportunity. Those of us who joined the parade were taught several new meanings for the word *use*. She didn't mind a little sweet agony, and she certainly didn't mind giving it. But no one I know would have had the courage or be crazed enough to kill her." Diana Merriam had started to slump in her chair but coughed and straightened her back. The detective's eyes bothered her. They seemed to be as piercing and knowing as Sandra's had been. Tru's practice of watching her every move and following every gesture in noncommittal silence made Diana nervous, while the lack of emotion or response to her statements unnerved her. The detective seemed hard, unpredictable, and predatory. She didn't look like Sandra, but she had the same veiled suggestion about her.

"You lived with her. She must have cared for you more than she cared for anyone else," Tru probed.

"I don't think that was possible. I cared for her. I was what she wanted me to be: willing, accessible, limber, and adventurous. Other than that, I don't think she cared for me or any other human being," Diana said, trying to move away from those piercing, haunted eyes. The eyes didn't seem to buy her attempts at banter or negation of regret. Tru's deepset gray eyes veiled their own thoughts and pulled Diana in. She felt open and disclosed.

Tru watched Diana Merriam. She saw the full range of her emotions, the control she was trying to maintain, and the fractures beginning to show in the sturdy buffers she'd erected to guard against contradiction. There were contradictions in tone, description, and the physical posturing. Tru sensed that Diana was close to the surface of her sentiments. A push here, a suggestion there laid out in the right way, and she'd tumble open like a broken lock.

"You are the sole heir to her estate. The restaurant, the bank accounts, the house, and some tracts of land in the Ozarks. That doesn't sound like bad intent, misuse, or disinterest to me," Tru countered, watching Diana's face.

"You must be joking," Diana said in wide-eyed disbelief.

"New will. The attorney said the ink wasn't more than two months old. Was she changing? Was time mellowing her and with it the way she showed passion and caring for you? Did that infuriate you, the idea of not being able to share in the plundering of other flesh? Was she getting boring? Or did you simply get tired of being her doormat and plaything? Did it make you crazy when she brought the younger, firmer Karen Bayborn home? Did it signal the repetition of old patterns and a final betrayal?" Tru taunted and pressed for the break.

"She did that? She made me heir to everything she had?" Diana Merriam asked in bewilderment. She threw her head back and stared at the ceiling, began laughing, and then abruptly cried. "She loved me, and I never knew? Never knew!" she cried openly, whispering her amazement over and over again. Diana's head bent forward as she drew her hands gathered to her face.

Tru looked at the heaving shoulders of the woman on the other side of the table, saw the grief straining Diana Merriam's face through the hands that supported her head. She saw the bewilderment, anguish, and bereavement begin to take its shape in Diana Merriam's bearing.

"What have I done?" Diana Merriam choked in torment.

Tru's head whipped around to the mirror and raised her eyebrows at it in question. She hoped the recorder had picked up that murmured hint of a confession. It fell on Tru's ears like the crumbling break in a wall. She was close now, close to hearing the rest of the story. Tru waited and let the full weight of the murder grind down on Diana Merriam.

My goddess, Tru declared to herself as she watched the breaking woman. This was the first time Merriam had let herself mourn. She'd been holding herself together in flippancy and audacity. It'd been a performance. Exposed for years, she'd have had to learn something from Sandra Vandamier after all. She had loved, did love the woman. For all the misuse that had been heaped on her, she'd loved Vandamier. She needed care, counseling, and time to recover, but she was malleable under the thin armor she'd grown. There would be some help for her in the treatment programs offered in prison.

The phone rang in the interview room, and Tru stared at it in disbelief. Phones were supposed to be switched off at the control desk when a room was in use by interviewing detectives. It rang again.

"Could be important, Detective?" Diana straightened herself, and teased at Tru.

Tru had a sinking feeling the moment was passing before her very eyes. Diana Merriam had been on the verge, a whisper away from confession, and it was slipping away.

"What!" Tru almost shouted into the phone, and made a cutting motion across her throat into the mirror where she hoped Garvan was still standing. She wanted him to make sure the phone was disconnected the minute she was finished.

"What did you say, again?" Tru stared at her feet and listened to the voice on the other end. "I see, fine. Thank you." Tru sat at the end of the table and looked at the notes she'd been taking while Diana had talked.

"Well," Diana quizzed, "was it important?"

"What time did you leave the house to catch your flight Sunday?"

"Wha—? Oh, around eleven, I guess. I was so angry with Sandra. We'd had a fight earlier in the day. I just had to get out of there. I left early so I wouldn't do something we'd regret."

"That was the lab downstairs. They completed the comparison of your prints with those found on the gun and bullets," Tru said slowly as she looked Diana in the eye. "The prints match."

"No, that's a lie! She showed me the gun when she bought it, but, I never . . ."

"You thought about killing her for a long time. You said so yourself. You had to build your nerve. One last humiliation, was that it? One last affront in the form of Karen Bayborn. Was that the final straw?" Tru pressed the issue hard at Diana.

"I — I hated her, loved her. She drove me crazy, but I . . ." Diana sucked air as tears began swelling up in her eyes again and her composed face cracked. She flung her arms across the table and hid her face.

Tru left the room, walked around the hallway, and into the viewing room. Diana was still sobbing as Tru watched her from inside the booth. The recorder was collecting the collapse, tentative admission, and disintegration of the suspect.

Something nagged at the back of Tru's mind.

"Nice piece of work," Garvan said heartily.

"Thanks," Tru said sullenly.

Chapter 9

Five A.M. found Tru sitting in one of her patio lounge chairs on the brief veranda of her second-floor apartment. She'd broken her self-imposed regime of smoking fewer cigarettes, and a ruby tip flared at intervals.

Tru had found the apartment a few weeks after she and Eleanor had split the sheets. She knew she'd been lucky to be searching for an apartment during the midwinter break at the campus of the University of Kansas Medical Center. It was an ideal location. She was a few blocks from her beloved Westport artist colony, party land, and food feast, and just five long blocks from plaza lights, glitter, and excess.

The second-story, two-bedroom apartment had been built at the end of World War II. It provided wood-grained grace, built-in bookcases, and a sense of air and light. Her gray cat, Poupon, had approved of the ready availability of pigeon snacks and shrub-lined curbs for hasty retreats. The balcony veranda ran the width of the living room and gave Tru a breezeway and relief from high summer. Tru didn't like air conditioning. It made her sneeze most of the time, and only the soft breezes of summer could carry the lush green foliage smells of her city.

It was quiet so far. Monday morning, and there wasn't even the wail of ambulance sirens on emergency approach to the Medical Center two blocks away. Large, well-shaped trees of oak, fir, redbud and pine dotted the curbs and miniature yards of the scattered complex. The beginning of the Westport district nestled a mere four blocks away down the short, rolling bluff past other multiple-family archi-tectural orientations. Even the Westport traffic had not yet succumbed to the breaking day and working-class threat of Monday morning.

Tru had closed the screen between the veranda and living room to thwart the entrance of pesky summer insects into her apartment. The phone had rung once, shortly before four-thirty. Tru had let the answering machine do its job. It had been Marki, asking her whereabouts and promising a night of delights if she would make an appearance. It had been inviting. But Tru had stayed put on the veranda. She sipped absently from her wine and silently apologized to Marki. Poupon lounged with her in the opposite chair and whisked his tail in irritation at her irregular sleeping habits. Occasionally he eyed her hopefully, then sighed heavily and resigned himself to her lack of consideration for his interests.

Snippets of the events of the night raced and competed for attention in her mind. A slithering sense of dis-ease snaked through her consciousness. It started after she'd returned to the interview room. Diana Merriam had been sobbing softly to herself, the worst part of the pain diminished into the typical hunch-shouldered, staring gaze of the guilty. Tru had seen that look repeat itself a thousand times before in that room. She waited to see if Diana Merriam would docilely offer to sign a confession, to admit everything, and slip a loose knot of liability around her neck.

Tru had called a stenographer in from the pool and set about preparing for the signing of a confession. She walked Diana Merriam through the procedure and began the questioning again. This time Tru asked for the exacting details. She probed for meticulousness of circumstance, for total recall, points of contact, timing, conversation, and the development of events leading up to the murder and Diana's flight to Chicago.

She made Diana Merriam walk through the scenes of the evening twice, and oftentimes more as she worked at ferreting out fact from fiction. Each time she thought she had walked Diana Merriam to the edge of confession, the woman would balk and step away. At four in the morning, Diana Merriam signed a three-page statement, not an out-and-out confession, and quietly asked if she could be shown her cell.

The request had surprised Tru. It surprised her

nearly as much as Diana's offer to sit through the grueling interrogation for the details of the case. Tru didn't like the look she saw in Diana Merriam's eye. The look was haunted, possessed, and distant from the world. The look was not a good sign. It signaled concern and alarm for Tru.

Tru requested a jail matron to escort Diana Merriam to booking and temporary detention. She took the officer aside and told her in a low tone that she wanted Diana Merriam on suicide watch over the next week and promised to sign the request sometime Monday. Events and questioning had dwindled Diana Merriam into fatigue, like a clock running down.

Attempted suicide by contrite confessors and guilty suspects was not uncommon in law enforcement. The strain of holding back, the emotional fatigue, and the pressure of culpability overwhelmed all but the most stoic or psychotic. To Tru's mind, Diana Merriam's face had taken on the haunted look of a potential depressed suicide candidate.

The department was thrilled. As far as they were concerned, Tru had all but wrapped up a high-profile and highly-volatile homicide investigation in less than forty-eight hours. The cooperation and complement of lab, pathology, detailed reports, interviewing process, and a perpetrator tied up in a bow combined to win her more points than she knew could exist. She'd been given the next day off, told to get some rest and let her assistants clean up the minor details. She had won the day. She would be allowed to ride that victory until the next hardscrabble investigation arose. Tru knew she should have been happy or at least content. But she wasn't.

Tru sat in the dark listening to whispers of

nagging suspicions and vague intimations babble incoherently through her mind. She tried to shake the feeling, but it persisted and nagged at her. Diana Merriam had talked. She told about her love for Vandamier, her hatred of her philandering ways, and the wish to see her dead. But she had not confessed. Diana had wound the rope around her neck, but she had not offered to tie the knot.

Tru scored it as a miss. And a miss in interrogations and interviews was as good as a mile. Tru didn't feel done, the case didn't feel won, and Diana Merriam's taking responsibility didn't sit right with Tru.

The sun was coming up as Tru poured another half glass of wine. Everything was all right, but it felt wrong. Was that it? Couldn't she take the pleasure of being able to do something without busting her knuckles over it? Everyone else had a little good luck now and again.

"Don't you think you deserve it?" she chastised herself. "What's the deal? I got the oldest story in the world going on. A lovers' quarrel turns ugly, a suspect breaks down like a cheap shotgun, and I can't stand it! Talk about fear of success," she snorted and knocked back a long draw on the wine. It sloshed over the rim of the glass onto her shirt, and she choked. "Damn it!" she yelled, frightening Poupon out of his slumber and back into the house.

"That's it," she said, carefully finishing the wine. She tossed the half-smoked cigarette over the veranda railing and stalked back into her apartment.

Tru decided to put it behind her, and the best way to do that was to go to bed. The slight buzz in her head from the wine promised to let her slip into sweet oblivion before the noises of the breaking day could disturb her.

As she slept, she dreamed of a woman with Sandra Vandamier's face and form slipping down hallways and taunting her with a wave of the hand. She flitted among the shadows through the curtains of doorways only to reappear somehow altered and sinister. In the dream, every step Tru took seemed to leave her farther behind the elusive Vandamier and the suggestiveness of her entreaties.

It was a restless and troubled sleep.

Chapter 10

At noon Monday Tru rose from her disturbed slumber and let the nagging irritations drag her through an abbreviated wake-up routine and back down to the department. It was at her. That pestering sense of the incomplete, the inconclusive. The signal she recognized as the cynic's warning system gnawed at her. She had no choice but to follow it until she beat it to death with sufficient information.

Face like a thundercloud, Tru sat at her computer console and typed out the details of the investigation.

She reviewed the reports, interviews with neighbors, Diana Merriam's statement, lab reports, autopsy, and business documents.

Tru knew that the first rule of any investigation was "it's not over until the perpetrator is sentenced," and up to that point it was all up for grabs. No investigation stopped because a suspect had been identified, arrested, and charged. That was only the first half of the war. The second half consisted of a long haul through the court system, defense attorneys, jury selection, and presentation of information. In the last half, anything could happen and usually did. The perfectly or near-perfectly assembled case could unravel like cheap cloth. The best facts, the best lab results, clear-eyed witnesses, and remorseful perpetrators could be rejected by the jury in favor of wild surmise. A system could buckle and break away under the minutiae of considerations. Expert witnesses could and would make fools of themselves and their professions through their differences of opinions. It was all up for grabs until the last *oyez, oyez* rang through the chambers.

"What's wrong with this picture?" Tru mumbled to herself.

On the computer terminal she typed FOR and AGAINST. *For* was for getting it right, for feeling good about the issue or item of evidence. *Against* was that which went against her grain, rubbed her the wrong way, and left questions in her mind.

FOR	AGAINST
DM prints on weapon	weapon belonged to Sandra?
DM passion motive	cash, papers, object(?) taken(?)
DM inherits estate	didn't know will changed recently(?)

DM gives incriminating statement	emotional trauma, grief(?), remorse(?) emotionally unstable — too easy
DM time and opportunity	could have been at airport waiting?
SV multiple affairs	no history prior to 8 yrs. ago?
SV bought business interest	where did she and money come from?
SV seductive, manipulative	controlling, secretive, anger issue(?)
SV money, desk, object	what was taken(?), why taken (?)
SV known in KC, community	who was Sandra Vandamier?

"What are you doing, North?" Gregory Bates's voice asked above Tru's head.

Tru started in her chair. "Cripes, Bates. Hasn't anyone ever told you not to sneak up on people while they're working?" Tru turned in exasperation and glared at Bates.

"Is that what you call that?"

"What do you want?"

"I thought you weren't supposed to be in today. I saw you sitting over here, hunched up to the screen like it was going to tell you something. What are you doing?" he persisted.

"Checking my facts. Don't they give that in Detective 101 anymore? And why aren't you finishing your paperwork on the Vandamier case?"

"Cute retort, and I am finished. Not much to do since you sewed it up last night. Thought I'd work on that Simmons burglary. I think I've got a lead over in the Quindero district."

"It's not done, Bates. The Vandamier case isn't finished yet."

"What do you mean?"

"Well, for one, where are the witness statements you were to have given me?"

"That? They're just a bunch of crap guesses from

103

neighbors. I don't think anyone was up at that hour. The uniforms didn't do much of a job keeping everyone separated. I got a fistful of half-assed I-was-asleep-but-I-always-knew garbage from the whole shitload of them."

"I need them anyway. There might be something. If not, I'll go back and talk to them myself."

"Christ on a crutch, what would you want to do that for? Don't you think I know how to do my job? You're the one who put me on that shit detail like I was some sort of damn rookie." Bates raised his voice in unveiled anger.

"It all has to be done," Tru said slowly. She didn't want him, or her irritation at him, to distract her from her intended focus. "You said yourself that the uniforms didn't do a great job in keeping people separate. Did you want to trust them to try to figure out what questions to ask? Imagine what a cluster that would have been."

"Yeah, and your point being?"

"Point being, if they can't do the little things, why trust the real issues to them? It's not their job. It's not what they've been trained for. Not yet, anyway. It's called division of labor. We do the detail because that's what we're paid for and trained to do, even if it feels unworthy of us. Got it?" Tru glared at him.

"That's one opinion, I suppose."

"Well, take the opinion and take it over to your desk and bring it back to me while you fetch those witness statements. OK?" Tru said in dismissal and turned back to the computer screen.

As she was printing off her list of FOR and

AGAINST she heard Bates return and toss the statements on her desk. She could feel his eyes boring into the back of her head. She didn't look up or give any signal or acknowledgment of his presence. He stomped off, muttering something under his breath.

"You're all sweetness and light," Tom Garvan stated in amusement.

Tru dropped her head into her hands on the desk. "Is it coffee-break time, or am I the only one with enough to do to keep me busy?" she asked in exasperation.

"Now, now. Jones told me you had a tendency to be a little temperamental when you put your teeth into a case. He never said anything about putting teeth into anyone who got within striking distance."

Tru sighed heavily and looked at Garvan. "OK, all right. I'll give you that." She considered her attitude and softened her approach. There was no reason to give Garvan grief simply because she'd decided to worry and gnaw the case like a dry bone. "Let's start over. What have you been up to this morning?"

"Well, now that you ask, I have a few things that may or may not help you put a blue ribbon on the package." Garvan smiled at her and turned to go back to his desk.

Tru had to chuckle at him. He sat in his wheeled desk chair and navigated a crawl back to his cubbyhole. He looked like a spider turned upside down, clicking and scrabbling along with the wheels of the chair propelling him in an awkward reeling motion. Garvan disappeared momentarily along the partition corridor. Tru could hear him returning on the same protesting wheels. In a flourish he bumped back to her.

"Garvan," Tru said, shaking her head in amazement at him as he placed the file folder on her desk. "You've never impressed me as a lazy man. Until just this moment."

He looked at her quizzically. "What? Oh, this?" he said swiveling in his chair. "This isn't lazy. This is play, but don't let it get around," he said, winking slyly at her.

"Play?"

"Yeah, play. I may be fast approaching fifty, but I take my play where I can find it. You should try it sometime."

"I don't —"

"It's simple," he said, lowering his voice to a conspiratorial whisper. "We get old when we stop playing. Or when we stop looking for ways to play, make sport, lighten up. This job, and I've had it a few more years than you, can crimp you, bend you, and warp you if you're not careful. And sometimes even then. So," he said brightly, "so I play, make it a game, put a top spin on it every chance I get. Even if it's something as silly as playing wheelies in this chair."

"And that helps? Helps you?"

"It hasn't hurt me yet. May not make me very promotable, but there are more important things than being at the top of this place's promotional list, sanity for one."

"Does your wife know about this?" Tru laughed.

"Do you know what the definition of an adult is?" Garvan asked, arching his eyebrow at Tru.

"I believe I do."

"I bet you don't. Really. I looked the word up once about twenty years ago. In Webster's unabridged it said that an adult is something that no longer grows, has ceased to grow, and having reached zenith is slowly working toward atrophy. Pretty scary stuff." He smiled.

"So wheeling around in a desk chair prevents atrophy?"

"Maybe not, but play slows it. Plus, I may have misquoted Webster's slightly." He winked. "But being able to be amazed once in a while, and finding ways to be joyful, keeps the juices going."

"You're a strange man," Tru remarked.

"Yeah. But when I retire, I'm not going to be one of those moldy old cops who goes out and eats his gun because he can't imagine anything else to do," Garvan said pointedly.

"And I would?"

"No, maybe not, now that you've been the recipient of my wisdom," Garvan concluded with a salute, and wheeled himself back to his cubicle.

Tru watched Garvan go in amazement. He'd always seemed steady and pedantic. Maybe it wasn't such a good idea that the department hadn't hired a new shrink after the previous one had committed suicide. It had been over six months. Sometimes troubled cops needed a little professional help. And perhaps detectives needed it once they started doing wheelies.

Tru dragged her thoughts away from Garvan and back to the task at hand. The list of FOR and AGAINST glared at her. She wondered if she were imagining things, trying to make the whole process harder on herself, or was there something to all the questions she had so carefully listed?

Tru spent the next hour gleaning details from the

materials Bates and Garvan provided. If she were imagining things, she felt confident that the facts would make themselves known. Tru knew victims' information was important. The why of a particular victim often gave clues as to the perpetrator. But this wasn't a case in which the perpetrator was unknown. Sometimes things simply happened to people, good, bad, or indifferent. It was a matter of lifestyle, time, circumstances, and myriad other events over which no one had any control. Perpetrators sought whomever for their own reasons. Greed and a love affair gone wrong were fairly typical and mundane. Still, Tru muttered to herself, Vandamier was harder for Tru to get a grip on than the reason for her murder.

According to information available from the will, insurance reports, and corporation documents for the restaurant, Sandra Vandamier was born January 14, 1951, in Kansas; an only child; both parents were deceased; no other known surviving relatives; social security number 511-00-5155; no major illnesses; no scars or tattoos; no military history mentioned; no criminal record mentioned; and she held a master's degree in business administration from the University of North Carolina, awarded in 1987.

"Garvan," Tru yelled over the gray barricades of partitions. "Anybody run Vandamier through the National Criminal Information Center?" Tru wondered if NCIC could give further light on the deceased.

"No need," Garvan yelled back.

"Right," Tru said at the computer screen as she coded in for terminal use. The query screen for NCIC asked Tru to provide it with a seemingly overwhelming amount of information about the requested name. Tru gave as much as she had. Sandra MIU (middle initial unknown) Vandamier. 01-14-51. White. Female. 511-00-5155. D. Brown. Brown. 165. All other blanks filled in with Unknown.

Tru was looking for probabilities of match. The NCIC computer would crunch away on the information and spit back one to fifty possibilities on the first run; the second run would give another fifty. It would give a probability of a match gauge ranging from one hundred percent to ninety percent. If she wasn't pleased, she would ask all other minor matches in descending order of percentage for examination. Tru hit ENTER, and the screen winked acceptance. Tru made notes to herself on Continued Investigation forms while she waited.

Three minutes later the screen chimed incoming information at Tru. NCIC advised that it had twelve possible hits. The likelihoods ran from ninety percent to fifteen percent. She scowled at the screen. She was a little irritated at herself. She'd thrown a pretty wide net with what she had available and had come up fairly empty. In resignation, she scanned names on the list one by one.

There weren't seventy Sandra Vandamiers in the world by any stretch of imagination. What NCIC had produced for her was a list of all white females with age ranges between forty and fifty who fit the general physical description within three inches, twenty pounds, with dark brown hair and brown eyes. Names ran a simple alphabet soup of possibilities. The name Sandra Vandamier didn't appear. It would seem that Vandamier was as crime free as Diana Merriam had been.

Three of the women listed were deceased. Ten of

the names had active felony warrants out on them, and one was noted as currently serving time in a Pennsylvania prison. Tru printed out the list with its detailed information and stuffed it into her briefcase.

Sighing heavily to herself, she entered the code for the North American World Wide Locator Network (NAWWLN). The NAWWLN would take the demographic and individually identifying particulars of an individual, scour lightly through military records, governmental agencies, banking records, and other forms of identifiers to find out the last known address or city of residence of an individual.

If anything came up as a possibility, and if Tru suspected that she was running hotter than the cold gut feeling she'd been betting on all day, she could check further. The databases would provide a complete history of places of residence for any one of the names she'd entered. She could trace movement from town to town and state to state over the life of anyone who paid taxes, voted, paid utility bills, had a bank account, served in the military, or ran afoul of the law. It was a long shot, and it seemed futile. However, the one thing Tru wanted to know now, almost more than anything else, was who and where Vandamier had been before she came waltzing into Kansas City, Missouri.

Tru knew that unknown and slightly dangerous qualities could be tempting and arousing in the first blush of intimacies. But in this instance they had become questions that she wanted to have answered in the wrap-up of an investigation.

Tru entered Sandra Vandamier and the list of women not noted as being dead or in prison from her NCIC sheet. Leaning back in her chair she watched the screen wink acceptance and decided to reward herself with a snack in the building cafeteria while electronics and microchips did their deed.

At three-thirty that afternoon, as Tru walked back to her desk, she could hear her phone ringing. As she sat, she glanced at the computer screen, noting that NAWWLIN had done its job and signaled that it was awaiting further instructions.

"Hello," Tru said absently into the phone as she punched the PRINT button.

"Tru?"

"Yeah?"

"Tru, it's Marki. What are you doing?"

"Oh, a little work. I had some things I needed to take care of. What's up?"

"An early supper. I'm thinking about sitting on the patio under the broad canopy of trees, ordering out from that wonderful little Vietnamese restaurant on Thirty-ninth, opening a tart little white wine, and letting the afternoon of the workaday world roll on without me. I was also thinking how wonderful it would be to have some company. Sound interesting?"

Tru looked at the paper in the printer chunk itself into a rolling pile in back of her desk. She glanced at the file folders she'd collected from the other detectives and wondered what she was doing at the office. She began trying to put the stacks back into some kind of order.

A sticky note dislodged itself from its tiny mooring and fell out of the pile onto Tru's shoe. Marki was still talking to her as Tru bent down to retrieve it. It was from Garvan's information and interviews in the case. A quick jot about a car Bayborn had seen leaving the cul-de-sac when she arrived the night of the murder. There hadn't been anything about it in the statement Garvan took from Bayborn. Tru speculated that it had been something Karen had said to him on the way into the office that night.

"Tru, are you still there?" Marki's voice sounded distantly.

"Yes. It sounds like a wonderful and interesting idea," Tru responded. The images of Marki, tall sensuous Marki, her blue eyes flashing under long luxurious lashes, full, firm, and conditioned body, with a sarong tied loosely and barely above the juncture of her breasts came flooding into Tru's mind. She was a treat to behold and a titillation to touch.

"What are you wearing?" Tru whispered into the phone.

She quickly sifted through the papers on her desk. There was nothing about the car Karen Bayborn had mentioned. It might be nothing. Some neighbor's late-night tryst, a teenager sneaking out of the house, a dedicated pizza delivery person. Then again, it might be something, but it wouldn't be anything unless she found the description. Tru practically growled, forgetting the phone near her mouth.

"Why, Detective North, what sort of question is that?"

"A very interested question. Do you have an answer?" She decided she'd kill or at least seriously maim Garvan later. She had to have that description. She found Karen Bayborn's phone number on her statement sheet and circled it in red.

"I see, well, what do you imagine I'm wearing?"

"One of those sarongs, the silky blue one, preferably."

"How clever of you. It just so happens that's exactly what I am wearing," Marki said, as she looked down at her tattered blue jeans and loose-fitting navy-blue top. She decided to change before Tru arrived. "How did you know?"

"A lucky guess, or somebody practices sweet lies. Which one is it?"

"It will be what I'll be wearing by the time you get here."

"By the way, if I go back to school and get my doctorate, could I work the hours you work, too?" Tru teased. She knew she had to get off the phone and call Bayborn, but she hesitated, holding on to the silkiness of Marki's voice a little longer. Priorities, she warned herself. Priorities.

"Only if you're very, very good at what you do and get to be the chair of the department. Other than that, I'm afraid we make everyone work at least twenty-four hours a week," Marki said, knowing Tru sometimes worked too long for her own good.

"Well, then, I'm not sure it sounds worth it. As it now stands, I put in fifty or so hours a week," Tru mocked.

"Come on over here and see if your academic aspirations are sincere or not."

"Be there in a few minutes. There're a couple of things I need to do here first, but I'll be there shortly. I might also bore you with some things I need to run past you."

"Really, as in . . . ?" Marki asked hopefully.

"Oh, this case, how the day has gone. I even

promise to let you do half of the talking. Like, how things are going for you and that sort of stuff."

"I see," Marki said, a little crestfallen. "As long as there's other stuff, as you say, then perhaps we'll see."

"Great, see you." Tru hung up the phone and hurriedly gathered her paperwork.

Chapter 11

"Can I help you do anything about dinner?" Tru asked as she lounged in a comfortable chair on the flagstone patio at Marki's house. Her mind felt like warm mush trilling away to itself after the last hour of making love to and with Marki.

"I'm just going to nuke it," Marki called from the interior of the house.

Tru sipped on the tall glass of iced tea and settled into the lazy relaxation of the day. Marki Campbell's fenced backyard was a wonder of English-garden taste. It seemed so incongruous to Marki in some ways. When Tru first met her, she'd been clad in the black jeans, shirt, and boots of a bouncer. She'd been playing a part to entertain herself and relive some aspect of her college student days, a time before she was a professor of psychology. She seemed to fit the stereotype. However, over the last several months Tru had learned that Marki was a very complicated, intriguing, multifaceted woman. She didn't fit anyone's stereotype. It would take some time to get to know all the ingredients that were part and parcel of the woman. Tru looked forward to the task with eagerness and only a slight twinge of trepidation.

"Here we go," Marki said, carrying out the tray of steaming food.

"I could have helped." Tru started to jump up and help Marki carry the tray to the covered patio table. She cleared the table of her papers and folders to make room for the meal.

"If your legs are as weak from the remaining tingles of voracious lust as mine are, I'm not sure you'd have been that much help," Marki said, winking at Tru.

"I know, but I couldn't help myself. There was that sarong, and you were in it . . ."

"Not for very long, as I recall."

"Why hide beauty?"

"You didn't want me to answer the door naked, did you?"

"No, but now that you mention it, it does conjure up an interesting fantasy."

"Are you trying to be suggestive?"

"No, I thought it was pretty plain."

"I'm curious. I think I see a pattern here, but

I'm not sure," Marki said, expertly using chopsticks to pick up the steaming noodles and beef.

"Pattern?"

"Yes, maybe. You're always a little intense, a little more than what most people would find comfortable. That intensity replicates itself, I'd guess, in the way you do your work. By the way, it also replicates, duplicates, and boils over in your lovemaking. But, when you're on a case, the seething, sexual tension seems to increase tenfold. Have you noticed that before?"

"I'm dull when I'm not working a homicide?" Tru asked, trying to understand and avoid the question.

"No. No you are not in the least. But that's not what I was talking about. I think you know that," Marki said as she bit down on the noodles.

"I can't say I've ever thought about it."

"Well, you are. Or at least I think that's the way it is. There's nothing wrong with it. It's simply intriguing, but I haven't got enough information yet to be sure."

"When do you think you'll have enough information?" Tru asked, eyeing Marki warily.

"Could take years? And, if those years are anything close to the last four months, it will be wonderful." Marki tried to lighten her tone and put Tru at ease.

"Speaking of things that could take time," Tru said, fishing into her file folders, "this case is beginning to get on what few good nerves I have left."

"How's that?" Marki asked, noting the avoidance and dismissal in Tru's behavior.

"It doesn't feel right. I think there's more here

than meets the eye. I don't know. Maybe I'm imagining things. See here," Tru said, waving a piece of paper in Marki's direction. "This woman, Vandamier, is as slippery as an eel. She drops in from out of nowhere. It's like she didn't exist before she came to Kansas City."

"How's that?"

"I ran her through NCIC, nothing. Then, out of curiosity, because I wanted to get a better feel for her and answer some questions about her background, I ran her through a big computer network. Nothing. She's not anywhere."

"So?"

"So? So you cannot not be in this net. I'm in this net. You're in this net. This net is linked into every computerized information system in the United States. I could find out where you were born, if you ever got a speeding ticket, bought a car, bought a house, defaulted on a loan, or paid a utility bill. We're all in this soup of data connections."

"You could find all of that out?" Marki asked in unpleasant amazement.

"Well, yeah. It would take some time for those details, weeks probably. First, the only thing it would tell me is that you were in there and some very cursory information about a few past cities of residence. The detailed search takes court authorization, an incredible amount of time, and no few bucks spent by the department. But your name would come up as long as you were born sometime in this century," Tru asserted.

"Then, although I'm not sure I like the idea of anyone being able to obtain all that information on me, what does this have to do with Vandamier?"

"She's not in there. I put in her name and all the significant demographics I had on her. She just isn't there. It's like she never existed," Tru said in frustration.

"She had to exist."

"OK. She does exist. From the moment she arrived in Kansas City, Missouri, she existed, but not a squeak of anything before that. You know, Diana Merriam said it was as if she'd been dropped off by a UFO. Vandamier never talked about her past even to her partner," Tru said, shaking her head in wonder.

"She's not the only one not to do that, Tru," Marki said pointedly.

"Well, some people say some things," Tru responded without hearing the inflection in Marki's voice or the accusation.

"What kind of people hide everything, don't speak of the past, keep it all to themselves?" Marki pursued.

"What? Oh, I see what you're trying to say. You think Vandamier had something to hide. No kidding," Tru said in light sarcasm as she smiled at Marki.

"No, seriously. If your network system is so absurdly connected and omnipotent, how would anyone escape it? Besides, no one hides forever. You said Vandamier surfaced here. She arrived eight years ago when she was thirty-seven. Surely no one reaches the age of thirty-seven without leaving some trace of a past."

"It's what you said. She had something to hide." Tru looked at the stacks of NCIC and NAWWLN papers again, her eyes wide in anticipation. "She was hiding. Who hides? Fleeing felons, people with more history than they want known, absconders from the

119

family nest, people who owe taxes, alimony, child support, and people who want to start over. That's who hides," Tru said as she sifted through the documents.

"Can they hide so well as to hide from your net?"

"Sure. There have been cases of it before. For example, about ten years ago there was this ex-Weatherman, you know, Vietnam War protests, militant, dangerous, into explosives, arson, and robbery?" Tru said looking at Marki for recall. Marki shook her head and shrugged her shoulders.

"Anyway, this guy was under for almost fifteen years. He surfaced. You have to surface because you have to have the basics: food, shelter, and clothing. I mean he really surfaced. He called the FBI and told them where to pick him up. Seemed as though he got tired of hiding and waiting for the long arm to snatch him up.

"You know what he was doing?"

"I can't begin to guess. Where does a militant arsonist hide?" Marki encouraged. Tru was getting excited by the hunt and the smell of the game. Marki watched and saw Tru's eyes glisten. She could see the wheels turning in her head as the experience and information aligned themselves in her mind. It was interesting to watch. The process was a lesson in animation, concentration, and deliberation. It was a rekindling of the intensity she had tried to explain to Tru. Marki stared at Tru wonderingly. In the middle of heat and light, the person who ignites never feels the flame, she surmised.

"This guy," Tru said, shining her eyes on Marki, "this guy was working for the federal government with a little subagency in the Department of the

Interior on some environmental protection project. He'd been living in Montana for twelve years and had been a federal employee for almost ten years. He hid in plain sight. Actually, he hid under the eagle's ass. That was why they couldn't find him. Funny, huh?"

"But how did he hide?"

"Jeez, I can't believe I've been looking at this stuff without seeing it," Tru said in exasperation.

"I'm only going to ask one more time."

"Oh, yeah, right. There's really only one way to hide. Absolutely. You have to do it absolutely, resolutely, and completely. No half measures, no fond memories, no reaching back. You go under and stay there, changed forever."

"Under and changed?"

"Whatever you were, whoever you were, you change completely. You go one hundred and eighty degrees from the life you're running from. If you liked country-and-western music, you never set foot into a hoedown dance hall again. If you were a college professor, you never take or teach another course in your life. For someone like you, Marki, you'd get a job as a laborer and never use your education again. Or, you could pay some bucks for phony credentials, but in something like anthropology instead of psychology.

"You would have to be prepared to do it for the long haul. You could never dare to call home to the old folks again, make contact with friends, former spouses, lovers. You'd wear your hair different; different color, cut, and style. Get some of those colored contact lenses, change your whole wardrobe, throw away everything that spoke to individual style and taste, and start over on the other end of the spectrum.

"You'd hide out for a while as a drifter. Stay out of trouble. Don't get stopped by the cops for anything. Stay away from trouble and troublemakers. You'd have to be a better citizen on purpose than most people on the planet. But that would take money or friends in on the conspiracy of reidentification. Stay down for a few years. Work your way back out into the light. Have your phony identifications for a birth certificate, a driver's license, diplomas, a social security card, training certificates, and whatever else you wanted or needed to give you a new lease on life. That's how you'd hide," Tru said triumphantly.

"It sounds impossible," Marki interjected. "That's a lot of work and trouble to go to."

"It is. Most people who try to hide don't do very well. They slip up, backtrack to old ways, old haunts, family, and friends. That's what an investigator is waiting for, the slipups. Changing everything is the only way to stay out of the way of the law-enforcement types that are looking for you. Even if they don't know they need to be looking for you, if anyone runs a check on a phony driver's license, it will come up stinking and you'll go to jail until they find out who you are. You can't hide unless you're very dedicated and very smart. It's not a game for children or double-digit IQs."

"Sometimes people just think they're smart and only end up fooling themselves," Marki noted.

"The old Weatherman Underground type did it. There have been other cases, few and far between. You know, there is no telling how much of that might

122

be going on. I know so few cases, and they're the ones who gave up. Hiding becomes a dedicated pastime. Actually, it probably becomes their life. Maybe that's why the old hippie dude needed to surface. Maybe he couldn't stand the idea of being a lie any longer. He'd remarried and had a family and children to think about. He may have wanted to be truthful with the people he loved and he couldn't be until he stopped hiding."

"How will this help your case with Diana Merriam?"

"I don't know. Probably it won't hurt it one way or the other. Who Sandra Vandamier was is not the point in the case against Merriam. If she killed her, and that's where everything seems to point, dead is dead and murder is murder."

"Why bother with this, then?"

"It's a burr. It makes the whole picture tilt out of focus. It might be the real motive as to why Merriam killed her. If I can get more information on this, it might be the key I need to make Merriam explain herself and confess the murder. With a confession and the material evidence, there would be no doubt as to guilt. The case would sail through the court system like ten pounds of Ex-Lax in a five-pound goose."

"That's attractive." Marki shuddered at the image.

"Not very." Tru laughed at the disgusted look the imagery had spawned on Marki's face.

"What now?"

"I need a conspirator. I need a little help from the good Dr. Houghin in the pathology department and ultimately the FBI."

"Is there anything I can do?"

"You already have, but why don't we go back

inside and discuss it," Tru said, reaching for Marki's hand.

"This is more of that intensity thing, isn't it?" Marki said wearily.

"Maybe. Why don't you do a little more information gathering and tell me about it, later," Tru said as she led Marki back into the house.

"I think we have a role problem here," Marki said as Tru gently pushed her down on the bed.

"Roles? You're into roles?" Tru teased the knot on the sarong.

"I rather thought I was supposed to be the assertive, aggressive one in this relationship. After all, I'm taller. I can carry your hundred and twenty-five bulk, I look better in black, and I seduced you first. That's a role," Marki crooned at Tru.

"Tell you what, we can take turns if it's that important to you. I'm taking mine now," Tru said as she ran her hands over Marki's hips.

"Dibs on next," Marki said, pulling Tru's down to her.

Chapter 12

At four A.M. Tru woke up to the feel of Marki snuggled against her back. She lay quietly, wondering what noise or sound had brought her to full-awake status. Her ears tried to stretch themselves as she listened intently to the house. Nothing stirred except the sound of Marki's deep sleep.

Tru shifted and gently moved Marki's arm from where it was draped across her. Marki mumbled and turned over to free Tru from her comforting hold.

Slowly and carefully, Tru sat up in bed and surveyed her surroundings. It was a large airy bedroom with southerly windows arching from ceiling to floor. The spacious queen-size bed seemed guarded by the tall posts at its corners. Marki had repainted and wallpapered the room in soft greens, lavender splashes, and gray trim. It was sumptuous without being prissy or overly strong.

Tru thought how well the bedroom suited and reflected Marki. A woman's gentle touch with an underlying strength and agile grace. It was an interesting combination. The right combination to make Tru feel more comfortable than she had felt in a very long time.

As she sat looking down at Marki's sleeping form, Tru's mind began to turn over the case she'd been working on. All the issues rose like haunting specters before her. Tru grabbed her head and tried to will into silence the questions, problems, and scrutinies connected to the case. Their whispers persisted and grew louder. It was no use. Tru knew the routine. Once her mind started churning and burning on an issue, sleep was no longer a possibility. Gently, she shifted her legs away from Marki's and eased herself out of the bed.

She dressed in the moonlight that flowed through the windows while she looked longingly back at the comfort she was abandoning. Downstairs she wrote a quick note of apology and explanation to Marki. Tru hoped Marki wouldn't be too angry or upset with her for leaving, but she had to go or risk tossing and turning them both into wakefulness.

Tru gathered up her files and papers and left the house. She arrived at her apartment shortly after four-thirty. Dashing up the stairs and through the back door, she grabbed some cat food from the refrigerator for Poupon, poured it in his dish, and headed for the shower.

Half an hour later she was clean and dressed for work again. She ran her fingers through her hair, still damp from the shower, and knew it wouldn't yield to styling until it was dry.

She didn't want to wait that long. The clues she needed to find out all about the real Sandra Vandamier lay in the file folders in the other room. She wanted to get at them again.

Then there was the question of the car Karen Bayborn said she'd seen leaving the area. When Tru had talked to Bayborn, Karen hadn't been very helpful. She wasn't an admirer of vehicles or their description. Bayborn had indicated that the only reason she'd noticed it driving out of the cul-de-sac was because of the peculiar markings. She described it as a canary yellow with paw prints on the driver's side door.

Tru had almost discounted the information about paw prints on the side of the door. Tru's car often showed paw prints across the hood, windshield, and trunk. Her gray Poupon made exploratory forays over it every chance he got. It was only when Karen speculated out loud as to why anyone would want to paint stupid designs on their car that Tru's ears perked up.

Karen told her that the car door had been practically covered with hand-size paw prints drawn on the door. She told Tru it reminded her of the gunned-down plane symbols she'd seen used in old war movies. A way of keeping score.

When asked if Vandamier had known anyone who drove a vehicle fitting the description, Karen had just laughed and said Vandamier wouldn't condescend to talk to anyone who drove bad taste. Tru thought it was an odd description. Blatant, overblown bad accents were something a juvenile from the fifties might do to sport up his car. But cat paws? Wasn't it supposed to be flames, speed waves or wild animal faces? Tru made a note for herself to request that district patrol officers keep a watch out for the vehicle. If nothing else, the driver may have seen or heard something that might be helpful.

She sat at her computer and entered all the identifying information of the women provided by NCIC and NAWWLN and the details she had available about Sandra Vandamier. She took a quick break and fixed herself some coffee at six o'clock and returned to her desk. Tru finished entering the information at seven and let Poupon out for his errands, then began to write her search program.

The phone rang at seven-fifteen and she answered it, knowing who would be on the other end.

"Tru?"

"Marki, did you get my note?"

"Yes. I'm just calling to make sure everything is all right."

"Yes, everything is fine. We're fine. I just couldn't sleep anymore. I was afraid I'd wake you. My mind started to run away with me, and I had to get back to work."

"You're the strangest creature sometimes. Do you know that?"

"You've mentioned it once or twice."

"Well, I was right. I have to get ready for work

myself. I've got an eight o'clock class today. Will I see you later?"

"I hope so, but I don't know what all I'll be doing today. I'll call if other things make me change my plans. OK?"

"That would be fine. Don't work too hard."

"Bye." Tru set the phone back into the receiver and smiled warmly at it. Sighing heavily, she turned back to the computer console and the program idea.

She'd entered twenty pages of identifiers with the names of the women provided by the information bases. Somewhere in there Tru hoped a key to Vandamier would appear. That, or it was a perfect waste of time, love, and Marki's warmth. She programmed to align the names for similarities, dates of birth within two years, social security numbers for fit with noted states of birth, known whereabouts within the last twelve, ten, and eight years. She included those who were reported as dead, missing, or wanted for a felony charge and presumed still at large. When she finished, she sat back and looked at the program. She was not happy. It was a messy program. It was a messy case, she insisted to the screen. She turned the computer program to the patterned search. She punched the enter key and set the electronic brain to spinning down its own little corridors and pathways.

Tru looked at the clock. It was nine-thirty. She was late getting to work.

She grabbed the phone as she poured a third cup of coffee.

"Bob Jones," she requested, holding her breath.

"Jones here," he said as the line clicked over to

his extension. "Who's this?" He had the air of a harassed man in his voice. He'd been made unit supervisor two months ago with his responsibility linking him directly to Captain Rhonn. It was not an enviable position for anyone to be in.

"It's Tru, Bob," she said cheerfully into the phone.

"Where the hell are you? Rhonn's been on my butt all morning about you. I gave you one day off, not two. I've had to lie and tell him you were knee-deep in tying up the details of the Vandamier case."

"You didn't lie. That's exactly what I'm doing. It's a hunch and a long shot, but I may have a way of finding out who Vandamier was."

"She's dead, that's who she is," Jones said, his tone becoming a little testy. Spending half of the morning warring with paperwork and Rhonn had left his generally cheerful disposition more than a little frayed. He'd been having more than a few serious misgivings about taking the promotion to unit supervisor. It was keeping him out of the field and neck-deep in the administrative details he'd always hated. He only took the promotion because it meant more money, but some things have other kinds of price tags attached to them.

"Look, Bob, the woman doesn't, rather didn't, have an identity until eight years ago. I think it may be linked to why she got killed. I want Merriam to crumple under the weight of information. If I can nail this down, I can get her to sign a full confession, with or without an attorney present. I'm sure of it," Tru chattered and exaggerated for a little spare time.

"You think so, do you?" Jones said, backing up a little.

"Yeah, I do. And if it doesn't work out, I'll give you the time I owe and your troubles with Rhonn in honest payback."

"Name your poison?"

"I'll . . ." Tru fumbled, searching for a deal that she could live with and that he'd accept. It was tit for tat in the unit, and it was better to make an offer than depend upon the kindness of even the best supervisor. "I'll work with Bates without complaining, too loudly, until they assign him to some other division. The caveat is that if they don't assign him in three months, the deal is off."

"That's a little thin."

"It's not that big of a favor," Tru said pointedly.

"OK. I'll cover for you. But be sure you come in with a good story in case Rhonn asks. Make sure you tell me what it is so I don't make a fool of myself," Jones admonished.

"You, a fool, it'll never happen."

"Right. By the way, they'll be arraigning Diana Merriam Wednesday morning at nine."

"I'll get with the assigned assistant district attorney later today."

"Good. They already have the paperwork."

"See you later." Tru hung up the phone and looked hopefully back at the computer as it winked and blinked its little working light. She chanted a small prayer for erratic programming and left her desk to fix a bite of breakfast.

After retrieving Poupon from his outdoor forays and her stomach somewhat satisfied, Tru decided it was time to bring in the necessary pathologist co-conspirator in the expanding investigation of the Vandamier case.

"Dr. Houghin?" Tru asked into the telephone receiver.

"Yes?" a distracted voice said on the other end.

"Dr. Houghin, this is Tru North."

"Oh, Tru, how are you?" Dr. Houghin's voice brightened.

"I'm quite fine, thank you. Doctor, has anyone come to claim the Vandamier body?"

"No, dear. Why do you ask?" Dr. Houghin pushed aside the papers she'd been working on at her desk and listened more intently to Tru.

"I was hoping they hadn't. I need a favor from you." Tru eased toward the conspiracy of inquisitiveness.

"What sort of favor?" Dr. Houghin leaned back in her large leather office chair and removed her glasses as though it would help her focus on what Tru was asking.

"I'd like to have you lift the finger and palm prints from the body," Tru said and held her breath.

"Really? What's going on?"

"I have this hunch, a little overactive imagination, or women's intuition." Tru cringed a little, remembering how Dr. Houghin would admonish a cadet class about the dangers of gut feelings and other unenlightened, nonscientific behavior.

"Can you be a little more obtuse, dear?" Dr. Houghin smiled into the phone. She remembered the bright, inquisitive, and smart way Tru had performed during her extended assignment to pathology. She was willing to help Tru in whatever way she could, but

132

the disciplined mentor side of her insisted that she make sure Tru understood the motivations and rationales of investigative directions.

"I'm sure I could," Tru chuckled into the phone. "All right, it's this. Sandra Vandamier doesn't seem to have a past. There is nothing in her documents, files, personal papers, or legal documents that say she existed anywhere before she came to town eight years ago. I find that a little unusual. Everyone, as you know, keeps some memento or more from places they've been and their life in general. Vandamier is a blank slate."

"That is curious. Could be she wasn't a sentimentalist?" Dr. Houghin cautioned.

"Maybe, or maybe there was something she didn't want to remember or have anyone else find out about. Either way, it may present a motive for her murder and give me a cleaner sweep in court with our suspect."

"If she were hiding something and you find it, it could also wreak seven kinds of havoc on your case. You never know what you're going to find."

"Yes," Tru said, running her hand through her hair. "But if I don't follow it up, if I don't find out what's hidden there, it could just as easily trip me up later."

"Good. I'm pleased to know you're still more interested in what the facts are and the truth, than just the opportunity to slap a case together. I suppose that once we get the prints, you'll want me to fax them to the FBI," Dr. Houghin said as she buzzed for one of her assistants.

"That would be the idea."

"That kind of checking could take weeks, Tru,"

Dr. Houghin said as she handed the responding assistant her note to lift the finger and palm prints from Vandamier's body.

"I'm hoping to narrow it a bit. If I can, I'll send you a list of names for them to check specifically. It won't be ready for a few more hours. If not, we'll have to ask them to be kind to us and do it the old-fashioned way, one computer-imaged comparison at a time in their multimillion-file system."

"They'll love that. It's not going to be a very high priority for them."

"I'll take what they can give," Tru sighed.

"I'll have the prints waiting for you, names or not. You call back and let me know which way you want to run with this."

"Thanks, I owe you." Tru sighed in relief. She didn't know where her search would lead, but she knew she had to go down that road to satisfy her curiosity.

"I would be willing to accept dinner at the Avenue Landing on the plaza as partial payment. I'd rather go to Phoebe's Phoenix, but I understand they've run into a little management problem," Dr. Houghin, said turning back to her papers.

"On my salary? What am I saying? Of course, it's a deal," Tru said quickly, relenting her hesitation.

"Later, dear. Save your pennies," Dr. Houghin said cheerfully into the phone before hanging up. She turned back to conclude the autopsy report on a fifteen-year-old male child who'd gotten on the wrong end of his gun-wielding, drug-dealing friend.

At the other end of the phone line, Tru stretched and decided to get a few quick winks before going to the one-thirty appointment at the district attorney's office. She felt exhausted. Her disturbed sleep and hours at the computer had conspired to make her feel drained. The only thing that drained her more was the idea of working with Bates for three months.

Poupon watched and ran after her to share the nap.

Late Wednesday afternoon, Tru sat in her government-inspired cubicle of gray and mauve partitions. The fluorescent lights hummed in near-silence overhead. The documents and reports spread out on her desk made her feel anxious and exhilarated at the same time. She had taken a wild-card interest in the peculiar past of one Sandra Vandamier, and the wild card was looking like it might have to be played through.

Diana Merriam had been successfully charged with second-degree murder at the preliminary hearing earlier in the morning. In plea bargaining, the district attorney had decided to go with second degree instead of first degree based on the contention the act was committed in a fit of passion, the murder weapon was owned by the victim, and the disturbing vacant presence presented by Diana Merriam.

The manslaughter indictment and its abbreviated rendition of the probable cause in the case sat atop the autopsy report Dr. Camellia Houghin had sent over to Tru in the late afternoon. The complete autopsy report lay on her desk. Her own photocopy was colored by yellow and blue highlighting marks. Dr. Houghin had detected that the trace skin and blood type found under Sandra Vandamier's fingernails did not match Diana Merriam's. The bruising on the arms suggested a grip strength and size that could not have been duplicated by either Diana Merriam or Karen Bayborn.

Tru looked from one document to the other, and the list of six names generated from her computer printout. A second copy of the names with their demographic and statistical details had been forwarded to Dr. Houghin on the return trip with her office assistant. Tru hoped that Sandra Vandamier's prints and the list of names were being faxed by Dr. Houghin to the FBI while she sat blinking perplexedly at the contradicting piles of paper.

Dr. Houghin had been right. Her nice clean case had just got messy. Someone else had been with Vandamier after Diana Merriam had left for her flight and before Karen Bayborn had arrived.

The court documents indicting Diana Merriam shrank in significance. Dr. Houghin's forensic pathology information made a reasonable doubt big enough to drive a semi full of jurors through.

Tru sat in stunned silence with the realization that she was fresh out of suspects, leads, and ideas. She could see the attagirl praise she'd won from command and administration fading into one big ahh-shit.

She picked up her file folders and documents and tried to walk casually to the door and escape from the building. Tru smiled sarcastically as she realized she felt a little like Scarlett O'Hara declaring to a persistent Rhett, "I can't think about that right now. I'll worry about it tomorrow."

Chapter 13

The downtown police station used by the various units and divisions — detective, lab, traffic, juvenile, motor pool, and detention — was a grand old five-story building with its fat haunches squatting on one-quarter of a midtown block. It was its own little city of bureaucratic cubbyholes, computer banks, evidence and document rooms, and steno and typing pools, as well as counters for citizen complaints and customer courtesy. The modernization of the interior and its high-tech applications were discreetly hidden by the nineteen-twenties granite and the ornate facade of the exterior. The exterior always gave the impression that Eliot Ness could or should emerge escorting a member of the old Irish mob or old man Pendergast himself jauntily sporting a black derby and cane.

The building had been remodeled to accommodate the 1990 Americans with Disabilities Act by installing elevators, ramps, automatic doors, and widened doorways. In keeping with the tenets of the act, the city fathers and mothers in political control had hired visually disabled persons to operate the building's cafeteria. The cafeteria offered hot coffee, real breakfast meals, lunches, snacks, and other delights, to the three hundred fifty city employees who haunted the hallways.

Tru sat at a small table in the cafeteria trying to get the song from *Annie* out of her mind. Her coffee soured in her mouth as the words *tomorrow, tomorrow, tomorrow* rang through her head. "Stupid song," she mumbled into the paper cup. She knew she was going to have to go back downstairs and talk to Bob Jones. She didn't have happy news to tell him, and she was hesitating for all she was worth.

At ten-fifteen in the morning, the cafeteria was all but deserted. Desk jockeys and support staff had abandoned it shortly after their routine nine-thirty-to-ten break periods. Tru was enjoying the silence. She knew it was the last few silent moments she would have after she told Jones and Jones told Rhonn that the Vandamier case had gone sour.

A tall, well-dressed man stood at one of the cafeteria entrances and scanned the room. Tru noticed him and thought he looked like an attorney who had lost his client. His tasteful gray suit, crisp white shirt, silk tie, and deep burgundy attaché case marked him as overclassed for most detectives. He looked directly at Tru and proceeded to walk briskly in her direction.

Although not one prone to slouching, Tru sat up straighter as he approached. He looked intent, and his steady walk was aimed right at her. Halfway across the room his face broke into a grin that did not reach up to his eyes. Tru saw no warmth or sincerity in the face, merely practice.

"Detective North?" He stretched his hand to her.

"Yes," Tru said, ignoring his hand.

"Detective North, good. They said I might find you here. Mind if I sit?" His arm waved at the chair across from her.

"Make yourself comfortable. Who told you I'd be up here?"

"A detective Tom . . . somebody. I'm sorry, I'm Special Agent Tony Trevors," he said as he found his identification wallet and showed it to Tru. It said FBI.

"What can I do for you, Special Agent Trevors?" Tru asked with increasing curiosity.

"You may not know it," he began, "but you've made some people very excited and very happy."

"How's that?"

He reached into his attaché case and pulled out several copies of faxes and a thick file folder. "Although my boss woke me up at six this morning to roll me out on this, I'm pretty happy too. It seems as though you had a fax sent with a set of prints and names to the bureau in D.C. yesterday. Is that right?" He grinned at her.

"Yes." She didn't like the grinning young man. There was a slick twitch about him and the eagerness of the newly commissioned. His personality didn't match the money he spent on the clothes he was wearing. She wondered how long he'd last with the FBI.

"Then that's it. That's what did it."

"Could you just tell me what you're going on about?" Tru said in exasperation.

"This. The prints you sent belonged to one of the names you gave us. I have to tell you, that list was pretty clever. It made the search smooth as glass, and bingo! We got her."

"Who? Which one?" Tru could feel victory sliding back into her hands.

Special Agent Trevors handed Tru the thick file folder.

"Susan Volth, wanted for the high crime of bank robbery about ten years ago in Belton, Texas. We've been looking for her since. If you've got her, we want her. The bank robbery will take precedence over whatever you're holding her on." He smiled his wide smile again.

So that was it. He was smiling and giving her the glad hand so he could slip his wanted bank robber out of the local lockup and haul her back to Texas. He'd get a share of the glory in her capture and Tru would get a fuck-you-very-much from the bureau for doing their work. It was a nice try, could have worked, but not this time.

"What's in this file?" Tru asked as she flipped it open.

"A gift, for the exchange. From me to you. It will tell you all about Ms. Volth. She's really quite the colorful character. If you hadn't picked her up, she was pushing for the bureau record for the longest time anyone has evaded apprehension on a bank robbery. Three more years, and she'd have made the grade. We don't like that sort of record. We're very interested in getting her back to Texas and very appreciative of your help."

"Special Agent Trevors, I'm afraid Sandra Vandamier aka Susan Volth isn't going to be going anyplace with you," Tru said flatly and flashed a grin back at him.

"Now, see here, Detective. The FBI generally gets —" Trevors's once pleasant face puckered with indignation.

"No, you see," Tru interrupted the abrupt change in the young agent's demeanor. "I won't keep you from her, but we do have her on ice."

"If that's supposed to be a funny, antiquated way of telling me you intend to obstruct my investigation, I'm not amused."

"No. It's my way of telling you that she's dead. On ice, as it were. In the morgue, sampled by the forensic pathologist who sent those faxes for me. And I think being dead is going to take precedence over whatever you had in mind for her."

"You've got to be joking," his voice fell to the table.

"No, I'm not joking. But, here . . ." Tru said, reaching into the breast pocket of her jacket. She took out a business card and quickly wrote on the back of it before handing it to the dumbfounded agent. "That's the number for the pathology lab. Give them a call. They'll tell you the directions, and you can go look at her if you want. See ya," Tru said as she rose from the table, grabbed the thick file folder Trevors had laid there, and headed out the door.

Tru read the file all the way down in the elevator, as she walked across the hallway, and all the way back to her desk. It was a positive identification. Twenty-three points of match on the prints made the former Sandra Vandamier the bank-robbing Susan Volth. *SV*, thought Tru. She had kept the initials. It was a minor point but an odd gesture for someone who hid as well as Susan Volth had.

She sat reading the file and details of the life story of a successful bank robber. If the formerly elusive Vandamier hadn't begun to give her heartburn about the case, she might have enjoyed herself.

Tru read with increasing interest. Susan Volth had been born in Minnesota and lived there for the first seventeen years of her life. The information indicated the family was poor, the father was an alcoholic, and that Vandamier/Volth may have been subjected to his drunken molestations. At eighteen she fled the family home when she married a ne'er-do-well by the name of Terrance DiMaio. DiMaio was a small-time hood, petty thief, and inept burglar. For most of the first five years of their marriage Vandamier/Volth spent most of it alone while Terrance did time in local county jails. There was the smell of frying pan and fire about the dead woman's life.

Sometime later the couple moved to Belton, Texas, where Terrance must have tried his hand at honest labor because there were no more reports or mention of criminal activity until the early eighties. Tru suspected that as Terrance got older, he'd got a little smarter and wasn't caught as often.

Tru was having a hard time trying to imagine the woman she knew as Sandra Vandamier as a happy little wife on the dusty prairie or oil-soaked soil of Texas. It was difficult to imagine the classy, commanding Vandamier/Volth ever living in a trailer.

Things must have gone along shakily for some time without being the picture of bliss that an absent criminal record might suggest. Vandamier/Volth started accumulating her own little criminal record. Bad checks, shoplifting, and prostitution, ending in 1980 with a six-month sentence on a prostitution charge.

Terrance DiMaio's record showed an ever-increasing number of DUIs, assault charges, and minor run-ins with the law during the early eighties. In late 1982, Terrance DiMaio was charged and convicted of a strong-arm robbery and attempted murder of a convenience store owner in Belton. He was sentenced to twenty-two years of hard labor in the Texas Correctional System. His wife visited once a week for a month and then simply stopped. In February of 1983, Vandamier/Volth filed for and was granted a divorce from Terrance DiMaio.

Susan Volth or Sandra Vandamier had robbed the Central Bank of Belton, Texas, a little over ten years ago. Belton was a small, dusty town with good people, oil, and enterprising ranchers surrounding the area. No one would have thought to look at it as a place where millions of dollars flowed, but Vandamier/Volth had apparently figured it out.

As Tru read the reduced-print police report and FBI investigation notes she laughed aloud. Vandamier/Volth had walked into the bank in Belton, approached the only male teller on duty, and quietly walked out with two hundred thousand dollars. Vandamier/Volth had always been buxom. Ten years ago, the firm roundness of perfectly shaped 36-Ds swaying seductively through the sheer pink cloth of her blouse had reduced the bank teller into a paralysis of ogling.

There had been video cameras in the bank. But the management, in a fit of economy, had ordered them turned off unless staff observed suspicious behavior. Unfortunately, the swaying, mouthwatering jut of those breasts did not alert the teller into feeling suspicious. They did have a short videotape of her exiting the bank. The picture showed a blond-haired woman from the back, an A-line skirt, three-inch pumps, and the faintest hint of the curve of her right cheek.

The blushing teller told the investigators he thought there was a gun, there must have been a gun. He could remember the scent of her perfume, the perfect roundness of the areolas of the breasts, the pink of the sheer blouse. But his eyes never managed to travel as far as an inch above her bust line.

He had her note in his hand. Her fingerprints were later taken from the note. No description, or none that might be tastefully broadcast, was available to narrow the search for the buxom bandit.

Vandamier/Volth had walked out of the bank into the blistering hot August of a Texas day and away from her dismal, destitute past. And, like the Phoenix part of the name she'd created for the restaurant when she took over from the fragile Diana Merriam, she rose, changed and renewed, to a very different life in Kansas City, Missouri.

It was a starting place for Tru, a raft of information to be used in the furtherance of the investigation about Vandamier/Volth. Back to Diana Merriam.

Diana Merriam might have some ideas, more information with a little more probing.

And then there was Terrance. Terrance was still in a Texas prison and more than likely a hopeful parole candidate in their system. He was available and might be interested in providing information Tru could use in locating the person or persons responsible for the killing of Vandamier/Volth.

"Once more into the breach," Tru smiled to herself as she walked toward supervisor Bob Jones's office.

Chapter 14

"Go over it so I can understand what you're saying," Captain Rhonn said, looking from Tru to Bob Jones, Tom Garvan, Gregory Bates, and Assistant District Attorney Allen Ruderick.

Captain Rhonn had requested that the ADA attend the conference and that Tru tell him the new FBI and pathology information. Ruderick sat quietly listening to the details, problems, and gaping rent in his case against Diana Merriam.

Ruderick was not a happy man at that moment. The congregating of involved personnel in the office had been preceded by a long, hot drive across town. The air conditioner in his car had expired two days earlier, and he'd not been able to take time off to get it fixed.

Captain Rhonn was not happy, either. He didn't like problems, especially after he'd sent a note to the assistant police chief briefly describing how well his team had worked together to solve the case. In the note he had reminded the assistant of how his decision to assign Tru North as lead investigator had been a crucial factor to the speedy success of the case. He'd taken his bows and it now sounded as if he'd have to make an embarrassing apology or figure out how to leave the load of responsibility with Tru.

"The fact of the matter, the most crucial aspect," Ruderick began, "is the point of contradiction between the prints on the weapon and the blood types. The defense will have access to that information. It's required access. The problem with it is that it opens the door to the question as to who killed Sandra Vandamier." He leaned back in the leather chair and wearily wiped his forehead.

"Diana Merriam had an accomplice. Why couldn't it be as simple as that?" Captain Rhonn offered, leaning forward in his desk chair toward the assistant district attorney. He wanted to save the situation. It was his job to paddle furiously when a boat was sinking.

"She hasn't said that," Tru responded.

"So, she's only hinted at her own culpability. Something she would have stated in fact and confessed if you knew how to go for the throat in an interrogation." Rhonn's eyes narrowed angrily at Tru.

"We've been over that a hundred times today. It's

not a confession because it's confusion. She thinks she's responsible for Vandamier's death. Her statement reads more like the remorsefulness of the significant other. That is what she is. She's suicidal. She blames herself for not being there, for not protecting Vandamier, for not seeing Vandamier's growing fear about some other issue. According to Merriam, Vandamier had become increasingly paranoid and anxious about something. That's why she'd bought the gun," Tru said. She'd gone back over the statements Merriam and Karen Bayborn had given her and reflected on the details in light of the information the FBI agent had brought to her. Vandamier's life was more transparent now, but there were still those dark places peopled by the past that Tru could only guess at.

"What the fuck," loudly retorted Rhonn. "That twisted bitch was humping her, and you make her, both of them, sound like some half-assed romance novel. Christ, Detective North, this Vandamier bitch was twisted as grapevines. Maybe she just got tired of eating pussy and picked up a man along the way to try to remember what normal is."

"I think it may have been a man, too. But not for the reasons you do. Statistically, women don't generally use guns on other women. They're not afraid of being overpowered. I think it was her past, some portion of it creeping up on her. Maybe the people or person who helped her hide out before she came to Kansas City wanted a share in her money and success. Based on what we know now about her past, it's the one thing that makes some sense," Tru stated flatly, trying to ignore her anger and stick to the subject.

"Well, that's a nice lead," Rhonn said, his tone viciously sarcastic. "What I think is that the bitch finally got what she needed and what was coming to her. Shit, she went out and picked up a little strange stuff. Strange for her that is. Got her something with balls on it, got laid like God meant, and then her live-in or part-time cunt came over and killed her for it. That's what I think."

"I don't see —" Tru began, her own anger thundering in her chest.

"No, maybe you wouldn't," Rhonn suggested hotly.

Tru looked at him in slow rage. He was dangerously close to making a statement about his suspicions regarding her life. She had to move and speak very carefully to him now. She didn't want to become his project for termination again. She'd slid past the last nasty encounter. She didn't want to worry whether or not he'd assign someone to shadow her to see if there was information worth gathering. He meant it as a threat and a not-too-veiled hint of intimidation. Tru took a deep breath to calmly level her response. She wasn't going to let a bully and tyrant dominate her life.

"As I was saying, I don't see what that would have done for her if she wanted to stay hidden. It's very likely she chose her alternative life as part of her new identity. Choice, design, or desire, it doesn't matter. Except to do other would have signaled a change and an incaution she had not previously displayed. She was under —"

"Yeah, she was under. Under, over, and on top of half the cunt-sucking, ass-groping lezzies in town from what the reports indicate," Gregory Bates joined the fray.

149

Tru looked at him in disgust. There didn't seem to be anyone with rank he was reluctant to shine up to. His attempted smooching up to Rhonn's fury at her seemed to be another manifestation of Bates's long line of inappropriateness in his chosen career.

"That's very instructive, Detective Bates," District Attorney Ruderick said quietly as he cleaned his glasses. "I think the point Detective North is trying to make, whether we like or agree with the life Vandamier led, is that something happened recently that put the fear of physical harm or fear of loss into her. That's why so many people buy a gun. It's a matter of either you go hunting for something or you're afraid that something or someone may be hunting you. And I think it's a line of thought worth following."

"How would you like to go about that?" Garvan interjected, attempting to further distract the combatants.

"Well," Ruderick began, "I'd want the captain here to let you and North go to Texas for starts. I think we've done what we can to look back at Vandamier's life from this side of the pale. So maybe it's time to start at the other end and find out if her ex-husband would be willing to share his thoughts on whom she might have been hiding with before she came to Kansas City. That's what I'd like to have done." He stopped, put his glasses back on, and looked at Rhonn.

"It's a waste of time, money, and effort for two detectives to go," Rhonn protested.

"Then send one. Send Tru," he said, nodding to Tru. "She's the one who made the connection with Vandamier and Vandamier's past. It's a long shot, but

I've got the trial on the docket in two months, and I don't like to be embarrassed with loose ends. The defense will raise the issue, and I want to be able to respond that we've covered every detail. If I have to go into that courtroom with these holes in my case, I'll do it. But those are all the holes I want. The whole thing still points to Merriam, but I want to make sure it points dead-on."

"But —" Rhonn stuttered.

"If there is nothing to it, if nothing more can be uncovered, Captain," Tru suggested, and hated the way she had to encourage Rhonn, "the DA will be able to suggest, perhaps the same thing you were suggesting. Simply that Vandamier was being a little greedy that night. Got greedy, got caught, and got even with."

It wasn't an unlikely scenario, not with Merriam's persistent contriteness over her lover's death. But it didn't ring right with Tru. It was risky and compromising. She told herself she had to remain dispassionate regarding the probable innocence or guilt of Diana Merriam. The case investigation had to go forward until it led to the guilty party. The right guilty party. Gut feelings aside, the case had to come to a conclusion.

"Think of it as money well spent, Captain. Your superiors wouldn't be comfortable knowing you were penny-wise and pound-foolish, would they?"

"Fine. Just fine!" Rhonn angrily capitulated. He was trapped. He'd have to let Tru go on her wild-goose chase or be accused of thwarting the entire investigation. Rhonn knew Ruderick would tell the story his way to his superiors. He had to agree to the direction of the assistant district attorney on his own or wait for a phone call from headquarters ordering him to comply. Whether Tru found anything would not be the issue. To be marked as reluctant to cooperate with the district attorney's office would mark him as difficult. Command had a longer memory than an elephant and Rhonn knew that difficult people didn't get promoted. They got moved to broom closets.

"Good," Ruderick said, rising from his chair. "Let me know how it goes, Detective North." He hesitated at the door, thought about the stifling heat he'd find baking the interior of his car, shook his head, and left.

Rhonn looked at Tru from under his brow-shaded eyes. "The rest of you get back to doing something constructive," he said, not glancing at Bates, Jones, or Garvan. "You get your butt on the first plane out of here and go talk to that fuck in prison. Do you even know where he's at?"

"Yes. I checked with the Texas Department of Criminal Justice. That's what they call it now rather than Department of Corrections. He's in a medium-security facility in Beeville, Texas. Wherever that is." Tru had called the Texas Department of Criminal Justice after she'd spoken with Bob Jones earlier in the afternoon. She didn't know then if she'd be going, but she wanted to have the information if the question was asked. She wanted to be ready to do the next thing and still was.

"Get it done and then get back here."

"I'm almost there now," Tru said as she walked out.

Over the next two hours Tru made what felt like a hundred phone calls to various sublevels of the Texas Department of Criminal Justice. Slowly but surely she wove her way through the contorted hierarchy of information and forwarding call tones to the warden at the Beeville prison.

Warden Johnas Emory had been very cordial. His slow, southern drawl was a thick molasses of pleasantries, curiosity, and acknowledgment of her informational needs. He advised Tru that he would assign a lieutenant of security to her. He said that the assignment would speed her meandering through his facility, ensure her safety, and guarantee staff compliance with her needs.

He said he looked forward to meeting her and wished her a safe trip. He'd intoned something about being pleased to help one of his little southern neighbors to the north and hung up. It had been a curious conversation. Tru felt as though she had never been so completely subjected to the epitome of what must have passed as a southern gentleman's behavior. It made her want to go over to the emergency room at the medical center to get a shot of insulin or adrenaline. She wondered if they could also give her some to go.

By nine o'clock that night Tru was packing her one suitcase for the quick flight down to Texas. She'd discovered new levels of frustration trying to make travel arrangements through the city's contract travel agency.

The earliest flight she could get was eleven-thirty and included the most torturous route imaginable.

Beeville, Texas, was in the southernmost portion of the state and was apparently the inspiration for the old joke about not being able to get there from here.

The flight would take her out of the Kansas City International Airport to the Dallas hub. There she had a layover of forty-five minutes before boarding for the next leg of the trip to Houston. She would then have another layover for an hour before the final hop to Corpus Christi. She would rent a car in Corpus Christi and drive north on Interstate 37 for seventy-five miles and then across State 59 to the town of Beeville, Texas. If she was lucky, she'd get to the prison gates by seven-thirty the next morning.

She'd told the warden she wanted to read Terrance DiMaio's prison jacket and talk with an officer or two before she met with him. In his continued deference he agreed that courtesy from one law enforcement official to another would surely extend to that confidentiality. He had, however, cautioned her to sit in a comfortable chair while she read the jacket because the written collection of DiMaio's disciplinary reports, misdeeds, and disruptive behavior covered his first eight years in prison. He mentioned that DiMaio's criminal record was extensive but that perhaps the social-work histories and routine psychological reports would be of value to her.

He asked for her fax number so he could send along DiMaio's rap sheet and the psychologist's report for her reading pleasure on the plane. As he finished speaking, Tru could hear him turn to someone in his office and direct them to send the materials to her. The fax machine in the office started whirring and chattering twenty minutes after the warden had told

154

her to have a safe journey. The sixty-page fax finished printing at eight-thirty.

Tru had looked at the pile of curled paper as it cascaded out of the fax machine's catch-tray and onto the office carpet. She wondered if she would ever get real sleep again or if the Vandamier case would go on forever, keeping her wired and in enforced insomnia.

Chapter 15

During the early stages of the flight out of Kansas City to Dallas, Tru reviewed the case file again. With the supplementary information, FBI report, autopsy report, and details gathered through the six days since the murder, the file had grown to a fat, four-inch stack of paper. She sat alone in her section near the tail of the plane and flipped through the material, hoping something would catch her eye that she'd not noticed before.

A little after one o'clock Friday morning, as the plane worked its droning way south, exhaustion overtook her and she put the reports away in her briefcase. She turned off the overhead light, reclined the seat, pulled the blanket up closer to her chin, and closed her eyes. The muffled thunder of the engines became white noise and hummed a lullaby through the wings, lulling her to sleep.

The trip was punctuated by landings, layovers, extended delays, fits of sleep, and the file. The extended delays weighed on Tru like boulders tied to her neck, making her ache for the comforts of a soft bed and Marki snuggled sleepily at her side. She drank coffee, hot and black, to revive her dwindling strength and faltering energy. Each landing was drawing her closer to the prison and through ever-shrinking cities. She looked at the phone at the back of the seat in front of her, thought of calling Marki, and then didn't.

In Corpus Christi at seven-thirty that same morning, Tru trudged through the car rental lot looking for the blue compact she'd reserved. The sun was an hour new, and already she could feel the promise of the dry flame of the day. Her neck prickled in the early desert sun and the breeze wafting in from sympathetic Gulf waters. Fifteen minutes later, and nowhere near the spot shown on the computer-generated map provided at the rental desk, she discovered that in Texas *compact* meant driving a Lincoln instead of a Cadillac.

She turned out of the airport into the Friday morning horrors of the Corpus Christi rush-to-work traffic. The languidness she had felt from the interminable flight was immediately replaced by adrenaline as she matched wits with daring ground aviators on Interstate 37.

In Beeville at nine-thirty, Tru found a clean-looking motel and staggered into her room. She called Warden Emory to apologize for her delay and beg off the morning meeting.

"My apologies, Warden. But I'm so tired from the flight and drive that I don't think I can keep my eyes open."

"You just rest there, little lady. We're not going anywhere, don't you know," he chuckled in the phone. "You just call us when you're ready. Sleep well."

"Thank you. I'm setting the alarm for one. It's my intention to be there by two-thirty at the latest."

"Whatever you want and need to do is all right by us. I'll let Lieutenant Miller know you'll be calling. Everything is here. Don't worry your pretty little head about a thing."

Tru sighed in exasperation and held her "pretty little head" after she hung up the phone. She didn't know if she could stand to meet the warden in person. It was everything she could do not to crawl through the phone and slap the saccharine, condescending arrogance off his lips as it was.

"Spare me," Tru pleaded to the goddess as she crawled wearily into the beckoning bed.

The medium security prison in Beeville housed twelve hundred felons for the state. It was a new, modern, and high-tech secured facility. It was a city unto itself. Eight hundred seventy-three staff members employed by the state of Texas and one hundred contract personnel maintained the twenty-four-hour, seven-day-a-week operation of the guarded community. Administrators, cooks, secretaries, guards, mechanics, electricians, storekeepers, teachers, social workers, psychologists, nurses, doctors, accountants, and vocational educators stood their shifts inside the razor-wired fences surrounding the brick-and-stone buildings.

Ten security towers, raised sixty feet off the flat Texas plain, were stationed at significant intervals. Inside, guards carrying high-powered rifles were meant to discourage any attempt to breach the contact-sensitive fence.

Reasonable force was the rule used to stop a man from climbing the barricade and fleeing to freedom beyond it. The inhabitants were dangerous, hardened, and captive against their will. "Medium custody" was a euphemism used by the prison system to suggest that a man seemed to have spent enough time under high security, behaved himself, followed the rules, and appeared reasonably accepting of rehabilitation. It meant that the inmates were less than five years away from completing their sentence. It meant that the prison officials had some confidence that the men would rather do their time quietly than be sent back to the reduced comforts of maximum security. It was all of that and not one thing more. The "reasonable force" admonishment directing the guards in the towers meant they were to shoot to kill, just in case the official pronouncement had been an error in judgment and just in case someone tried to escape.

* * * * *

At one-thirty on Friday afternoon, Tru North entered the confined world of the Beeville medium security prison complex.

"Detective Tru North?" A smiling uniformed woman with lieutenant bars extended her hand.

"Yes, you're Lieutenant Miller? I'm a little earlier than I expected. I hope you don't mind," Tru said and shook the hand offered to her. Tru noticed the lieutenant's tan-lined face and noted that it was an interesting, revealing map of experiences.

"Yes. I'm your escort. I have to ask you if you are familiar with prison hostage policy?"

"No. I've sent a few people to prison, but I can honestly say I've never been inclined to visit one."

"Well, then, you're in for a treat."

"What is your hostage policy?"

"Simply put," Lieutenant Miller cocked a smile at Tru, "there are no hostages."

"Oh. That's impressive. Does that mean you don't expect the situation will ever arise? Are you that confident, and forgive me for speculating, but are you that confident in your security measures?" Tru wondered at the boast.

Lieutenant Miller laughed lightly. "We have every reason to be confident of what we do here. What you'll be walking through is the latest in prison design, operation, security, and technological security wonders. But that's not what I mean."

"Well, I did notice the fence, wire, and cameras, and I am wearing my identification badge the gate control officer gave me," Tru said as she looked about the area trying to see what other technological mechanics the Lieutenant might be referring to. She imagined pressure-sensitive devices, cameras too small to see, and monitors hidden in buildings.

"There are no hostages because it's not allowed." Lieutenant Miller guided Tru through a third electronic-gate barrier into the interior of the complex. "If you are taken hostage, our policy is we simply ignore it."

"I beg your pardon?" Tru halted before the fourth set of heavy, slow-moving sliding doors.

"If you are taken hostage, and if they try to use you as a bargaining chip and threaten to take your life to get us to comply with their demands, we ignore it." The lieutenant turned to Tru and smiled with a wicked grin.

"You ignore it? You're telling me you would let them kill a hostage? Me, for instance, in your example?" Tru asked, not liking the way the conversation was turning or the glint in the lieutenant's eye. Tru decided that if it was a joke, she wasn't amused or enamored with Texas humor.

"Yes, we'd have to. But we promise we'd get even. There are no hostages because we don't recognize hostages. The inmates know that. It's part of their orientation when they arrive. It's a standard operating procedure throughout the United States, as a matter of fact," Lieutenant Miller said soberly. The winning smile was gone.

"Right." Tru let the idea soak in. It was difficult. There were barbs and spikes coating the facts as surely as the razor wire glinted on the perimeter.

"It has to be that way. You see, if a visiting inmate's family, official visitor, or member of the staff were taken hostage, it would be the same. No hostage. Hostages, in the distant past, were sometimes used by inmates as bargaining tools. Officials complied, sometimes excessively, to try to win the safety and freedom of the hostage."

The fourth set of doors slid shut with a clang. Their hammering certainties of her extraction from the free world jarred into Tru's nerves. She felt as though she was beginning to understand the phrase about going into the belly of the beast as much as she ever wanted to. Fresh paint, clean floors, and bright lights aside, the pervasive strangulating confinement of the setting invaded her senses.

"Experience has taught us, hard-won experience, that hostages taken in a prison setting pose more risk to the quelling of the situation than not. They remain at risk for their safety and freedom until the incident is resolved. No inmate, no hostage-taker in a prison setting, is really in control. It's mob rule. A promise made is not necessarily a promise kept. And we can't afford to bargain the safety of the whole community, here or beyond these walls, for the sake of a hostage.

"It's the thing that weighs against the hostage. Your safety for the safety of every other citizen. It is very Dickensian. The needs of the many outweigh the needs of the few," the lieutenant said as she unlocked the door to a secured conference room. A booth with bulletproof glass was at the end of the room. Next to the phone on the table nearest Tru, a thick file folder strained its six-inch bindings.

"I think I appreciate your candor, Lieutenant, and I have to tell you I look forward to walking back through those gates again. Real soon."

"That's a normal response, Detective. If you work here long enough, you get used to it."

"Somehow, I don't imagine I'd feel quite that way."

"Really. You're as safe here as at your mama's bosom."

Tru didn't remember any steel, razor-slitting wire, or reinforced concrete anywhere near her mother's bosom. Looking at the lieutenant, Tru realized again why it took different people to do different jobs.

"The file is on Terrance DiMaio. The warden said you wanted to read it. It looks as though it will take some time. Call me at extension 453 on that phone when you're ready to see DiMaio. He's not been told you'll be here. We try not to tell the inmates more than they need to know about the operation of the facility. I'll have his corrections counselor bring him in on the other side of the interview cubicle," the lieutenant said, turning on her heel to go.

"Can you tell me anything about DiMaio?" Tru asked.

"No," chuckled the lieutenant. "There are over twelve hundred male inmates in this facility. I have four supervisors, fifty officers, and four support staff who report to me. I'm lucky to remember who I've assigned to what detail and when, Detective. We have specialists who deal with the inmates, contractors who educate or train or analyze them. I'm a low-level bureaucrat. I try to make sure the wheels stay greased."

"Thanks for the tour and information," Tru said, trying to imagine what it took to keep the rigid village operating.

"Call me. But don't go wandering around outside this room. When you're ready to leave, call me again and I'll come get you. The warden said he'd like to meet you before you leave. And since you're not used to corrections protocol, I'll tell you that his requests are always considered mandates."

"It would be my pleasure," Tru said, giving the lieutenant the required bureaucratic verbal compliance salute.

Tru sat and leafed through the massive folder for an hour. The file suggested that DiMaio was a nasty piece of work in and out of prison. She was still skimming the extensive social-work history when the door into the conference room opened.

"Detective North," the lieutenant said, as she walked into the room followed by an officer with corporal stripes. "I'm afraid we owe you an apology."

"How's that?" Tru said, looking from the lieutenant's face to the burning cheeks and averted eyes of the Corporal.

"Terrance DiMaio. He's not here."

"Not here? Has he been moved to another prison?" Tru felt her heart fall in distress to her stomach. She had a quick vision of herself driving across the wide plains, hills, and dales of Texas in search of Terrance DiMaio.

"No. He's assigned here. Tell her, Geberth," the lieutenant directed the corporal.

"I'm his corrections counselor. I didn't get the message about your arriving until this late this morning. I was going to mention it to the lieutenant but I got busy with another inmate. One thing led —"

"That's not getting to it, Corporal," the lieutenant said sternly.

"He's gone. Left around noon. He's on furlough. But he's scheduled to be back here Sunday evening at six sharp." The corporal looked into the file folder to check his information.

"What?!" Tru growled. She cursed silently. Every time she thought she had a handle on some portion of the case, it slipped away from her. She was getting tired of Vandamier/Volth or whoever the poor dead thing was supposed to be. She wanted some answers, needed some answers, and now.

"Furlough. He's a minimum security by exception. So he gets furlough leave if there's a family emergency. Other than that, he gets leave every three months for a weekend. Its part of our rehabilitation program to see how fit some of the inmates are for returning to a productive, law-abiding lifestyle," the corporal explained through his misery.

Tru's head swam in a haze of confusion. "Where'd he go?" she asked as the pounding headache crept into her temples.

"Home. His mother is ill. That was the emergency."

"Where, how?" She pictured the consternation on Captain Rhonn's face. She'd have to stay over in Beeville for the weekend. It wasn't the vacation spot of her dreams.

"Drove, I imagine. Took his car from the inmate lot and drove home. I'm really sorry about the inconvenience. If there's anything I can do to make —" the corporal offered.

"He had a car? Here?" Tru said in amazement as

she looked questioningly from the corporal to the lieutenant and wondered about the security boasted by the prison.

"We have about a hundred inmates in the faciliity who are considered minimum security by exception. Their behavior and cooperation with prison policy for two years make them eligible for consideration. Terrance DiMaio has been one of those exceptions for a year. If a man has a car or other transportation he owns, we let him park it in a secured lot. Terrance DiMaio has a car. It seems reasonable he would have taken it to go home to see his ailing mother," Lieutenant Miller explained in a soft, solicitous voice. She was poised to take the brunt of any belligerence Tru might offer. She was a bureaucrat of the old school, ready to take the blame to protect superiors and subordinates alike.

"What kind of a car? Where does his mother live?" Tru asked as warning bells clamored wildly in her head. The hair on the back of her neck stood up, and she felt the ancient reptilian segment of her brain grab her civilized, rational mind. It was like an electrical conduit ramming excessive voltage up her neck. She knew better than to ignore it.

The corporal consulted his file, pulled out a Polaroid, and gingerly handed it to Tru.

Tru stared at the glossy, colored photograph. A smiling man in dark-green gardener work pants and shirt leaned casually with his arms crossed against the side of the bright yellow 1982 Pontiac. It was the rally sport model with a spoiler on the back. It looked like it was the last car he'd owned in his free life and it had been cared for, babied, and pampered. The only thing that marred and spoiled the car's otherwise pristine features was the driver's side door. Fifty or more large paw designs marched across the door's panel.

"What are these marks on the door?" Tru asked, feeling the world spin away and slam back into her again. She held the picture up for the corporal, who glanced at the picture. It was tumbling into clarification. Vandamier's rising fear, the weapon for protection, and the violent struggle that ended her life illuminated Tru's mind like the lights in a fire-hardened diamond.

"Oh, that. DiMaio is a bit of a braggart, but then most of the inmates are around here. Those are his conquest marks. There's another fifty or so on the other side running down the length of the car," the corporal said, coughing. His face turned a bright shade of crimson as his eyes dropped to his booted feet to study something on the toes.

"Conquest marks? Let me guess," Tru said dryly.

"You'll probably guess right," the corporal said, fascinated by his shoes.

"It's the women he claims he's screwed?" Tru wondered what sort of little memento he'd design for killing a woman.

"Yeah, except every toe's supposed to be one woman. He calls them *pussy tokens*."

"I need a photograph of him, as recent as you can get. I want to keep this photograph for the time being. And where does his mother live?" Tru asked, rising from the desk. She was two to three hours behind him, and a lifetime if he was making his escape.

"It's, let's see, oh yeah, 921 Florence in Zapata, Texas," the corporal offered.

"Where the hell is that?" Tru imagined fleeting images of old western towns, wide-brimmed freedom fighters, bandoliers, and the turn-of-the-century war between Mexico and the United States. Viva Zapata. Tru heard the words ring and wondered if the community had been named for the fiery, legendary rebel.

"About two hundred to two hundred and fifty miles from here. A spit across the Rio Grande from Mexico," the corporal responded nonchalantly.

"What's going on?" Lieutenant Miller asked.

"I'll try to explain on the way out." Tru walked beside the lieutenant and corporal through the long series of gates that were there to protect the rest of the world from known bad intent. Her heart beat furiously in her chest. She realized that if her luck held out and continued the way it had been going, Terrance DiMaio would live to a ripe old age, safe and secure in some quaint little hamlet in an obscure Mexican province. She, on the other hand, would have to start thinking about another line of work before she boarded the plane back to Kansas City.

The next thirty minutes were hectic. Tru explained her case as quickly as she could to the warden of the Beeville prison. He asked careful questions. It was maddening, but she watched the wheels turn in his mind as he considered the extent of her speculations. She was asking a lot of him. She wanted him to broadcast an all points bulletin to the Texas Highway Patrol and the Zapata town marshall. The request meant no little sacrifice of the image of the prison to local law enforcement. And if she was going to try to tear down the highway to the edge of Mexico in pursuit of a potential murderer, she was going to need a weapon. She asked for one from his arsenal.

"I didn't travel with a weapon. As I am sure you are aware, the airlines won't even allow police officers to carry them on board unless they are escorting a prisoner. Frankly, most don't do that because they figure there's nowhere for the poor sod to run at thirty thousand feet," Tru advised the warden.

"I realize that. I have officers who escort revoked parolees all the time. They don't go armed. But you are asking a great deal," he said as he spread his hands plaintively toward her.

He didn't look like a warden should look as far as Tru was concerned. He was somewhere on the far side of fifty. He had thinning hair, a belly expanding to give his feet shade, and was wearing what Tru believed to be a habitual lopsided grin. It was his creamy complexion and soft, enfolding handshake that made her wonder about the stereotype she carried in her head. All the old movies, and new ones she'd seen, portrayed wardens as big, burly, sloping-forehead types, a smidgen above the criminals they supervised, and sometimes deadlier. This man was suited, cordial, and gave the impression he'd be more comfortable behind the loan desk at the bank.

"Look, I've got to ride this thing through to the end. I need a weapon, preferably an automatic. I have to find out if he went to his mother's." Tru felt her voice begin to increase in volume.

"And what do think the chances are of that?" Warden Emory asked pointedly.

169

"Slim and none. I figure he's confident he has a three-day head start on anyone looking for him. He's not concerned about police from Missouri or anywhere else. If he did murder his ex-wife, he took what he could get from her that night to top off his extortion money, came back here, settled in and waited for an excuse to leave. Mama called and he, with your blessing, took off."

"If there's an APB out on him, what do you think you can do, little lady?" The warden eyed her caustically.

"Tell you what. I want your help, so I'm not going to tell you how much I hate the term *little lady*. It grates on my nerves and makes me want to break something off," Tru said. She rose from the chair. "If he did commit the murder, and if the papers find out that you refused to assist me, I wouldn't put any money on the likelihood of your being able to retire from the Texas Department of Criminal Justice, Corrections, Prison System, or whatever you call it."

Warden Emory looked at Tru with steady, narrowed eyes. He said nothing. Tru realized she couldn't tell if he was breathing. She wondered if there was a training session in diplomacy she should have taken at the academy.

"Take Geberth with you," Warden Emory said, and turned to Lieutenant Miller. "Go to the armory and issue them a couple of the .45 automatics and extra clips. Give Geberth here a mobile phone. I want to know how badly he screws this up for us, and I want to know immediately. Geberth, you got like a whore's chance in church to come out of this with your stripes. But the only way you're going to get a

chance to do it is if you go with this lit — the
detective here, and try to be of some help. Are you
up to it?" the warden drawled viciously. Tru saw the
hardened, made-for-television warden momentarily
peek out at Corporal Geberth.

"Yes, sir," Geberth said, almost saluting.

"And Geberth. Take a rifle. You, your mama, nor
I know what you might find along the road.
Dismissed," Warden Emory said, scattering the
corporal and lieutenant to their duties.

"Thank you," Tru responded to the warden as
they left.

"And you," Warden Emory said, leveling his gaze
on Tru, "you take care of that boy. He's twenty-two
and my daughter's fiancé. She'd want him back here
in one piece, and I like to keep my little girl happy.
Understand?"

"Completely," Tru said as she left to follow
Corporal Geberth to the armory.

Armed with two Smith & Wesson Model 59
semiautomatic pistols and a Remington .30-.30 with
scope, Tru and Geberth headed to the prison motor
pool. Corporal Geberth signed for the vehicle, and
they climbed into one of the white Pontiac chase
vehicles in the facility's fleet. The car sported a light
bar of red, white, and blue strobes, a prisoner's cage,
radio, and the numbers 871 painted in bold black
paint across the roof. To Tru it looked like a patrol
car in everything but the name on the side of the
doors. "If you've got a radio in this thing, why did
we need a mobile phone?"

"Because," Corporal Geberth grinned, "Texas ain't
near as flat as she looks. The dips and hollows out
here will break up the radio signal. Besides, we'll be

out of radio range to the facility about fifty miles or so down the road."

"How long will it take us to get to Zapata?" Tru asked as she heard the engine under the hood of the car wind up. It rumbled and growled with greater power than Tru knew came in the standard police package vehicle.

"Why, this here, ma'am, is a chase car. We call it that because we can chase and catch anything as long as it doesn't have wings. And that's what we're going to do right now. Go for a little chase," Corporal Geberth said as he opened up the dual cam V-8 and spun out onto the highway.

Tru fastened her seat belt and promised herself she wouldn't look at the speedometer unless the vehicle started to lift off the pavement. Tru had visions about the grease spot she'd become if they hit anything bigger than the tumbleweeds that raced them down the fence lines. Grease spot, hell, Tru snorted. The sun baked the pavement and scalded the sky in Texas in July. She resigned herself to becoming a boiled grease patch if her worst fears were realized.

"How long?" Tru asked.

"Oh, sorry, ma'am," Gerberth said as he drove under Interstate 37 and south on County 59. "At this rate, I guess we could expect to be in ole Zapata in a little less than two hours. Give or take five minutes," he said, pronouncing Zapata as *Zee-pay-tea.*

Tru sat back and tried to figure out how she was going to manage to relax with the child at the wheel. The warden had told her she was to bring the boy back unscathed. She didn't know how she was going to manage that while she was captive in three thousand pounds of steel, the speedometer needle pegging the post, and a wild grin of excitement spreading across the corporal's face.

The Texas landscape flashed by. Hundreds of innocent insects became goo and slime on the windshield, and Tru tried to imagine what it would have been like if she'd stayed in college long enough to get her teaching certificate. She remembered she didn't like children all that much and felt fairly certain the fates were kind but had a streak of amused derangement in them.

She opened the file folder on Terrance DiMaio and stared at his face. She wanted to take him safely back to Missouri. They'd walk, she thought, as she looked at the earnest speed demon next to her.

DiMaio had become lankier over the last fifteen years in prison. The arms sticking out of his short-sleeve shirt spoke of hard lean muscle. He'd been honing himself in the prison yard and gym. Dark brown eyes hid under a wide forehead and bushy eyebrows. The smile on his face seemed to hint at the successful blackmail he'd realize and the murder he contemplated once he located his ex-wife.

She sat back and waited for disaster or Zapata, whichever came first. She closed her eyes and chanted a relaxation mantra she'd heard several months ago. The near sleeplessness and nerve-contorting pandemonium of the last twenty-four hours caught up to her. She fell into her dreams.

Chapter 16

"Fucking son of a bitch," Terrance DiMaio cursed and jammed his busted bleeding knuckles into his mouth. The wrench he'd been using to break loose a rusted engine bolt had slipped. The knuckles on his left hand had slammed hard into the hot, unyielding engine block. He stomped around the side of the car and cursed the hot Texas sky. In disgust he threw the wrench in the direction of the rest-area toilets.

"Just be that way," he said as he kicked dust at the car and stomped over to the thin shade of the lone rest-area bench. He sat down and reached for the warm beer he'd started after he had managed to get his overheated car to roll into the dusty roadside park.

He tilted back the beer and cursed his bad luck. Everything had been going fine, and then the radiator hose busted. He'd been able to fix that temporarily with a little electrical tape and wire from his tool kit in the trunk. But fifty miles later the damn engine had begun to heat up and sounded like it would explode if he didn't stop.

"Every time, every, goddamn time," he muttered as he tossed the empty can into the scrub brush and reached into the tiny cooler for another beer. He looked at his watch and wondered how long he would have to wait for the engine to cool and get over its contrary nature or for him to get a ride to the next town. It was three o'clock in the afternoon. If his luck didn't change, he figured he wouldn't be in Zapata till dark, if then. He'd told his mother he'd be on time for supper. He had a few things for her, and then he'd head for the border and make Texas just another bad memory. He knew his mother would understand; she'd told him often enough that a fresh start would do him good.

"Fresh all right," he smiled to himself. But it wasn't as fresh and clean as he would have liked it. Susan had screwed things up for him again. He could have gone the rest of his life squeezing money out of her, making her pay for her disloyalty, and making her pay for treating him like a piece of garbage.

"Stupid bitch," he spat and crushed the can in anger. It had been her fault. Everything had been going so well. She'd been coughing up money like a magical wishing well. God, he loved to remember the day and the look on her face when he'd come waltzing into that high-tone eatery she ran. She'd nearly passed out, and the wide-eyed shock on her face almost made the risk he'd taken by using his furlough time to leave the state of Texas worth it. He knew that if the prison officials had ever got wind of his little forays out of bounds that he'd have been locked down tight for the remainder of his sentence.

Six months worth of extortion was all he had to show for his trouble. Thirty thousand dollars. But it was enough to let him live like a king in Mexico. He knew he would have to be satisfied with it. The stupid bitch had ruined everything. She'd told him she was finished with him. She'd said she was concerned that he couldn't keep his mouth shut, that he'd screw up and get her sent to prison. He felt angry remembering the night his golden goose died.

"I told you I'd see you tomorrow afternoon," Sandra Vandamier said as she swung open the door to her house. She glared at Terrance DiMaio in open defiant anger.

"Shut up, stupid cunt," Terrance said as he tried to shoulder his way past her into the house. When she held tight to the door and blocked his way, it surprised him. "What's with you?"

"It's late. I'm expecting company, and it's not you," Sandra said as she started to close the door.

"Company?" Terrance said, seeing her for the first time. She was dressed in a lavender nightgown. "Jeez what kinda company you expecting, *Susan*?" A leer spread across his face.

"That's hardly your business. Go back to your sleazy little motel, drink some more of that cheap beer, and wait till I call you tomorrow." Sandra Vandamier eyed him with contempt.

"Shit. You think I don't know what you've turned into. You think I don't know nothin' about your perversities. I think I'll just join you two sweet things. I always wanted to see what it would be like to fuck a couple of you queer pieces."

"Get out. You're drunk and a fool. You'll get your money, but this well is about to run dry. If you're still here by the time my guest arrives, I'll call the Texas authorities myself." Sandra shouldered the door and tried to shove him out of the way. The door stopped as Terrance rammed his foot between it and the frame.

"That's a hell of a threat. You do that and I'll tell them all about you. They still want you, you know. You'd be a lot longer in the clink than I would," he said as he tried to casually light a cigarette and lean against the barely opened door. She was a strong woman, and his toes ached in the pinching pressure she maintained on the door.

"It stops, Terrance. It stops tonight. You've got everything you're going to get from me." Sandra reared back with her weight and started forward to crush Terrance's foot.

"Like hell, it does." He'd seen the grim look of determination spread across her face. He reached through the door and grabbed her by the hair as he slammed his shoulder against the door. The force of his body against the door bowled her back as he swung into the room still clinging to her hair.

"We don't have to wait for company darlin'. I think I'll just rip me off a little piece right here and now." He grabbed her left arm and twisted it up behind her back as he shoved her toward the stairway.

"No." Sandra struggled, fell, and was dragged across the carpet until he collapsed on her.

"You can do this easy or hard, wifey," he snarled at her as he roughly picked her up and shoved her down onto the banister.

"I'm not your fucking wife," Sandra protested and tried to swing at him with her uninjured right arm. Her hand swung wide and grazed the tip of his chin.

"You are tonight," he said as he slapped her across the mouth. He grabbed her and dragged her up the stairs, pushing and shoving when she didn't move fast enough to suit him. In the bedroom he shoved her down on the bed and stood above her watching as she wiped the blood from a split lip. He stared about the room in awe and pleasure.

"This is some fine little love nest you got here." He grinned at her and began to unbuckle his pants.

"Wait, wait. I do have a guest coming. She'll be here any minute. You don't want to do this. You want money, that's all," Sandra said, desperate for escape.

"Yeah, meaning?" Terrance's hand stilled on his belt.

"I've got cash. Here. Lots of it. Jewelry. Things you can hock. It will make you richer than you've ever thought. But you've got to go before she gets here."

"You were going to dump me."

"I, no, it's, it's been, I've been confused since you came back. I'm in hiding. New life. New ways. Your coming back has been a shock, that's all. I haven't been able to adjust very well. You know how I am; it takes me a little time to get used to things, that's all. I don't want to go to prison."

"So we're still partners?" he said, eyeing her suspiciously.

"Of course we are. Hell, you don't think I could have written you a letter and told you where I was, do you? What kind of sense would that make. The law would have gotten us both."

"Yeah. Then what was all that hate spat downstairs?"

"You started it by coming here tonight. We were supposed to meet tomorrow. That was the deal, right?" Sandra said as she sat up on the bed.

"OK. We're still on, then. Just like before. Five thousand every time I get furlough. Right?"

"Yeah. Each and every time."

"But, wait a minute." Terrance leaned over Sandra, reached around her head, and grabbed her by the back of her hair. "You told me you had a wad of money here. Where is it?"

"Downstairs, in my den. There's a false drawer in the desk and a safe. There's fifteen thousand or more there and some of the jewels I mentioned. It's yours if you simply leave. But you have to go now," she said as she felt the fingers in her hair begin to relax and release her.

"What's the combination?"

"Fifteen right, forty-seven left, and fifteen right again."

"Well, what are we waiting for? Let's go get it and then I'll go." Terrance smiled at Sandra and hitched his pants up in confidence.

"Sure, just give me a minute. I want to wash my face."

"Going to make pretty for company?" Terrance sneered.

"Something like that," Sandra said as she walked toward the bathroom. She splashed cool water on her face and gritted her teeth at her reflection in the mirror. When she returned to the bedroom Terrance was lounging on the sheets.

"Real comfy here darlin'," he said and winked at her.

"It is, isn't it," she said, as she walked to the side of the bed and sat down next to him. She turned toward him to block his view of her hand as it reached for the drawer in the night table.

"You sure we don't have time for a little quick something?" Terrance asked as he raised up to kiss Sandra.

"Maybe something a little quick," Sandra said as she pulled the gun from the drawer.

"Stupid bitch," Terrance said as he put up his thumb and hoped that the trucker would stop for him. Stupid woman had tried to kill him. They'd fought over the gun. He'd been surprised at the strength and fury of her. Then the gun fired, and Susan had slid wordlessly down to the floor. Surprise and shock riveted him where he stood, and then panic overwhelmed him. He tore through the room, emptying drawers as he went, ran downstairs, and found the safe.

He'd stuffed the money, papers, and a little gold statue in his shirt as he ran to the back patio doors. Trotting across the backyard, he saw the gate and walked back to his car down the darkened side of the house. Nothing and no one stirred in the neighborhood. As he pulled away from the curb he tossed the statue on the floor of his car just as the lights of a car pulled into the cul-de-sac. Panic preyed on him all the way back to Texas and his mother's house.

Terrance watched as the semi slowed and pulled over to the side of the road.

"Where you goin'?" The trucker's sunburned face grinned down at Terrance.

"Randado, I guess. Got to get somebody to come back here and tow my car in," Terrance said, as he climbed into the truck.

"Run into some bad luck?" The trucker chatted as he pulled away and back down the highway.

"A little. But things are beginning to look up again. They got a station in town. I figure that will do the trick," Terrance said as he relaxed against the bench seat and let the air-conditioned cold air of the cab wash over him.

"I'm sure it will," the trucker said as he shifted up the gears.

Chapter 17

"Damn!"

"What! What!" Tru snapped out of her dreamy
fantasy at the sound of panic and alarm from a voice
near her. It took her a second to remember who
Corporal Geberth was and why she was with him.
Her eyes darted to the road, expecting impending
catastrophe.

"Damn it all to —" Corporal Geberth expanded.
"I'm sorry. I didn't mean to wake you up. You look
like you needed the rest."

"Thanks. What the hell is wrong?" Tru searched frantically inside and outside the car for the problem.

"Well, ma'am, I didn't check the gas gauge before we left. We gotta stop for gas or be pushing this car into Zapata late tomorrow."

"You must be kidding?"

"No, ma'am. I surely wish I were."

"Where the hell are we?" Her voice rumbled threateningly in his direction. She wondered who the warden's daughter would marry after she killed the young man sitting next to her. Tru figured the warden might even accept the idea once she explained how she did it in self-defense. Hadn't he tried to kill her by driving this rocket across dry land?

"We're coming up on Randado. That's only about thirty miles from Zapata."

"Whatever," Tru said slowly through her teeth, and reached for the mobile phone. She dialed information and got the number to the marshall's office in Zapata. She dialed the number and listened to the low buzzing tone ringing through the air.

"Zapata Marshall's office. Can I help you?" A woman's pleasant voice drawled out the sentence, managing to turn it into a whole conversation.

"This is Detective North with the Kansas City, Missouri, police department. I'd like to speak to the marshall."

"I'm sorry. He's stepped out for a moment. Shall I have him call you when he gets back from the barber?

"The barber? Can you tell me if he's located a car or the person of one Terrance DiMiao?" Tru didn't know what to do with her astonishment at the diligence of the marshall, so she internalized it and fell hard against the back of the car seat in indignation.

"Not that I know of," the voice answered sweetly. "Can I get your number?"

"No, no. That's all right. Maybe I'll stop in and see him if I get to town." Tru hung up the phone. She tried to convince herself that Zapata was a wide spot on the road with no more than five hundred souls to its name. No one could hide there. Furthermore, she thought, warming to her hope, if the marshall had read the teletype, he'd have known whether Terrance DiMaio was in town or not. He'd know it by simply looking down the dusty street.

She rounded out the fantasy as they pulled into the weather-beaten gas and vehicle-repair station on the edge of Randado, Texas. Tru stared at the building in disbelief. It looked just like the clapboard gas stations she imagined existed in the dust-bowl days of the thirties. She expected to see a young Henry Fonda walk around the corner of the sagging building at any minute. The large, two-stall garage and workshop snuggled against the back of the building. Tru wondered who in the world would trust their car to a station that couldn't afford neon. The only thing that seemed remotely contemporary was the soft drink machine. It stood on the far side of the station at the corner where the garage seemed to sag.

Corporal Geberth practically jumped out of the car before it came to a halt in front of the two lonely pumps.

"I'll be quick, I promise," he shouted as he ran

into the screen door, bounced off it, and opened it to go sheepishly inside.

"Don't worry," Tru said, and waved after his vanishing form. Don't worry. It was a long, worthless shot in the dark. Stupid even. If Terrance DiMaio was anywhere at all, he was already in Mexico, Oklahoma, Arizona, or some other plane of existence, Tru dejectedly conceded.

Corporal Geberth had turned off the car's engine when he almost brought the car to a halt at the pumps. The sun bore in on Tru and baked a fine glaze of sweat on her skin. She was thirsty and tired. She looked longingly at the drink machine.

Geberth bounded back out the station's screen door without falling through it and waved to Tru.

"We'll be out of here in a jiffy," he said, grinning to her as he put the gas nozzle into the car's tank.

"Whatever," Tru said. She got out of the car to stretch her legs in the direction of the drink machine. She had long abandoned her jacket to the backseat of the chase car but didn't figure she'd scare any of the locals with the holster slung across her back or the exposure of the revolver nestled under her left shoulder. It was Texas, and guns were in vogue.

She caught sight of her reflection in the dusty sweep of glass hiding the darkened interior of the dilapidated station. She thought she looked frightful, or maybe just a little pathetic. Her once sharply-pressed shirt looked as though it had lost a fight with a twister, and her slacks sagged at her knees from the hours of sitting.

She shrugged at her reflection and fished in her

pocket for the change she hoped she still had there. She was looking down at the coins in her hand when the man walked around the edge of the building. She didn't see him, and he obviously had not expected her.

They crashed together. His weight and height won the encounter. Tru bounced off. She forgot her loose coins and reached out to steady herself against the first thing she could grab. He responded in kind. The automatic responses of reaching out to keep from falling kept them momentarily upright, surprised, and distracted at the force of their collision.

In four seconds eternity slowed to a crawl in the dust at their feet.

Tru looked up into his face, and he felt his hand graze the revolver strapped snugly against her side. She stepped back a fraction of an inch and saw the gun stuck in his belt, wedged between the bright silver buckle and his shirt. He saw her eyes go wide. He looked up and beyond her to the Beeville State Corrections chase car sitting at the pumps. The young corrections officer was concentrating on his task, oblivious to the tangled promenade a few feet away. Tru's hands tightened on his arms, and panicked electricity surged through him.

Terrance DiMaio brought up a bruising right hand, hitting Tru hard across her upturned jaw. The slamming backhand forced a cracking moan from her lips as the force of the blow sent Tru flying backward and then crashing to the station's dusty, cracked cement.

Corporal Geberth saw the violent motion out of the corner of his eye and turned to see the scowling, hate-filled face of Terrance DiMaio as the man reached for the gun at his waist.

Tru rolled up to a half-crouch as she reached for her revolver, drew, and fired through dust-clouded eyes. Two explosions pounded her ears. She saw Corporal Geberth spin, bounce off the trunk of the car, and fall soundlessly to the ground. Relieved, she watched as Geberth's legs pulled and pushed their way around the far side of the car.

"Get out of here," she yelled to him. "Radio for help, but get out."

The last she'd seen of the dark-green-clothed Terrance DiMaio was his legs churn as he dashed around the corner of the station.

"Call the police," Tru screamed at whoever was standing in the station as she scrambled to her feet to run after the fleeing figure. She ran out of the sunlight and into the dark garage. She crouched inside the doorway against a large, stinking oil drum, listened, waited, and tried to glance over the interior. The dust in her eyes and the sharp contrast between the outside brightness and the shadowed garage momentarily blinded her.

She raised her eyes to the rafters, to the extended car lift, and almost had to suppress a confused giggle. There on the car lift, eight feet above the pavement, rested the bright yellow Dodge with its brag lines of cat paws. An exhausted radiator leaned mournfully against the lift post.

"Give it up, Terrance," Tru commanded. "You've got nowhere to go and nothing to get there in."

A shot rang out and struck the oil barrel she hid against.

"Shit," Tru breathed as she scrambled to new safety. A door opened suddenly at the back of the shop and flapped in the wind. Dust billowed up, signaling the likelihood of Terrance DiMaio's low, fast-crawling exit.

Tru crouched. As quickly and cautiously as she could, she made for the back door. She leaned against the dried planks of timber of the door frame, knowing their rotting bodies would give her no protection from the penetrating force of a bullet. She glanced down at the dirty cement floor and saw a wet stain pool at her feet. Tru gingerly touched the patch, raised the discolored tip of her finger to her nose, and smelled the sweet, iron scent of fresh blood. He was wounded. Her shot had not missed him.

Gathering her courage and foolhardiness around her, Tru squatted runner fashion and prepared to propel herself into a rolling landing out into the bright Texas sun.

"Give it up yourself, law lady," a harsh voice laughed behind her.

Tru's heart collapsed in her chest as she slowly turned her head and saw the lanky form of Terrance DiMaio in silhouette at the entrance of the garage. He hadn't gone out the door. He'd hidden in the shadows and waited for her to get stupid. She chastised herself. The dark figure raised his gun at her and waved at her to stand up.

"Might as well toss that piece away. Looks like I'm going to need a hostage, and you'll do just fine," he chuckled.

Tru stood up and raised her hands. She clutched

the pistol and remembered what Lieutenant Miller had said at the prison.

"I said, drop it and get over here." Fury tinged his voice.

Tru glanced around, hoping to find a point of salvation, a few precious moments and a way out of her predicament. She sidestepped down the side of the wall, her hands raised and the pistol gripped in readiness.

"Now you toss that gun over here or I'll just kill you where you stand. I don't want to do that, honestly. I ain't never had me no law lady before. And you look cute as a dumpling," he said, walking under the chassis of his car and menacingly closer to Tru.

"No, I bet you haven't," Tru whispered at him as she inched down the wall.

"Now, stop. You can't get out of here alive! Don't think you can outshoot me either, girl. The littlest flicker of your wrist I don't like will get you dead."

"Woman to you, asshole," Tru countered.

"Toss it, bitch, or I'll put one through that nasty mouth of yours. Now!" he screamed.

Tru took another step, stopped and let her shoulders drop noticeably. "All right, just don't hurt me," she said plaintively.

"That's better. Just toss it toward me. Real nice like," he said as he dropped his gun arm.

"Here it comes," Tru said. She dropped her hand, grabbed the lever protruding from the wall, and pulled it down.

Terrance DiMaio had just enough time to glance up before his face kissed the dropping frame of his car. The lift mechanism burst in a whoosh with the exhaust of escaping hydraulics as it slammed Terrance and his car onto the garage floor. The car bounced twice against the greasy floor; not as far the second time as the first. Tru didn't look to see if Terrance bounced twice too.

She holstered her weapon and walked out into the hot light of the Texas sun.

Chapter 18

Early Sunday afternoon, while Marki Campbell was busying herself with laundry chores, she heard a clatter and screeching of wrought-iron chairs on the flagstone of her patio. She picked up her portable phone and made ready to punch the preset number for the police if she found vandals or burglars at her back door. Carefully, she went to the French doors of the garden area and looked out. She saw Tru North sitting under the sheltering patio umbrella smoking a cigarette, with a half-gallon cooler sitting beside her.

"I almost called the police," Marki said as she slid the patio doors open and called accusingly to Tru.

"Don't bother, they're here." Tru waved cheerfully at Marki.

"You scared me to death," Marki complained, still carrying the forgotten phone in her hand.

"Come on outside and join me. It's not too hot yet."

"What are you doing here? I didn't think your flight got in until Monday afternoon," Marki said as she bent to kiss Tru's upturned face.

"It was Saturday night when I called, right? I had another one-and-a-half days to spend in Beeville, Texas. Oh, it's a fine little place, but then there was the thought of that horrible flight back. And all those terminal waits. So I became terminally impatient. I cashed in my reservation, rented a car for less than the flight back, and drove like the furies."

"You're kidding," Marki said, sitting down. She noticed the tomato juice glass in Tru's hand and the extra on the patio table.

"No, I'm not. Between being in Beeville and driving all night to get home, I chose driving. It's not their fault, but I've had all of Texas I care to for a while."

"What's in the cooler?"

"Bloody damn Marys. Want me to pour you a glass?"

"What's going on with you? What happened down there?" Marki asked in concern.

"Not as much as could have happened. The upshot is that Vandamier's ex-husband killed her. We found the money, bearer bonds, a statue, and a personal diary of hers in his car. He'd stuffed it up

192

under the trunk's insulated sheeting. Apparently no one at the prison ever searched the vehicles for anything other than weapons. I guess it makes sense. They weren't worried because they always strip-searched the inmates returning from furlough for weapons and drugs. Anything in the cars, trucks, or other vehicles was not accessible once they were out of the secured lot and back inside the fence.

"Seems as though DiMaio had been blackmailing and fleecing her ever since an ex-cellmate of his transferred to Missouri parole after he got out of prison. I didn't know until the other day that states trade parolees like sports stars, for a player-parolee to be named later. Seems as though they do it if the inmate has family and the possibility of a job in the lucky trade state. Anyway, as things would have it, he hired on as a busboy at Phoebe's Phoenix. The guy had remembered DiMaio bragging about his wife and had seen a picture of her that DiMaio had shown him. He wrote and told DiMaio what his ex was doing. Even sent him a newspaper photograph of her that had been in the *Kansas City Star* a year or so ago when she attended a major social event."

"So this guy was in on the blackmailing?" Marki asked.

"Doesn't look like it. He's still working as a busboy. I think DiMaio was furious with him. This guy essentially told DiMaio he was a liar and a fool for letting her get away. You usually don't thank people for that sort of observation."

"Didn't the prison officials know about the letter from another inmate?" Marki wondered.

"No. It's not part of their policy to read the inmates' incoming mail. In fact, they only read the outgoing if they have probable cause to believe that a crime might be being planned or committed. I've learned more than I had hoped to know about prison operations in the last few days. I understand what they do, but it gives me no small comfort." Tru sipped her Bloody Mary and reflected on the no-hostage rule.

"What about Diana Merriam?" Marki asked, reaching for the glass that had been offered to her. The idea of sipping a Bloody Mary under the shade of the wide umbrella held greater interest for her than the waiting laundry.

"Oh, they turned her loose sometime Saturday. Or earlier, once her attorney got wind of the Texas situation."

"Incredible. But, then, did Vandamier buy a gun to kill him?"

"No, I don't think that was the plan. I do think she was afraid of him and for just cause. He was violent, had a temper and, according to the reports I have, he used to use her as a punching bag when they were married.

"I think she panicked when he threatened her with physical violence. He was getting greedier in his blackmailing, and she was probably becoming more uncertain as to the extent of his vindictiveness. She had a lot to lose other than just money. Bank robbery would have netted her a sentence of twenty to life, and not the sort of life to which she had become accustomed." Tru looked up through the spreading branches of the maple tree and blew out the smoke of the only cigarette she'd allow herself until much later that evening.

"It all seems so strange and sad in a way," Marki said, shaking her head.

"You just never know. It's the littlest things that happen. They seem random, unconnected to time, place, or circumstance. Sometimes the threads aren't very visible, even with perfect hindsight. It's as though Vandamier set the thing in motion with the bank robbery, then buying controlling interest in the restaurant, and going public with her new persona. Then she hired a dishwasher, who of all things had served time with her ex-husband. Her ex-husband is cooling his heels well enough to earn furlough, like a good little felon, and his mother unwittingly helps him get an emergency leave. One little issue after another. One little moment balled up on another, and the whole world Vandamier had constructed unraveled itself."

"She took a lot of chances, and they finally caught up with her," Marki observed.

"She lied, hid, was angry, and never really shared herself with anyone else. That's sad, too. I know it sounds out of character to feel sorry for a felon, but her whole life wasn't what you'd call pretty."

"You think it would have played out differently if she'd opened up somewhere earlier on?" Marki asked, wondering where this line of conversation would take Tru.

"Maybe, but she would have had to start real early. But any time is better, perhaps, than not at all."

"Meaning?"

"Meaning we probably have some things to talk about," Tru said, glancing at Marki.

"Like what?"

"For starters, when does summer school let out? Next week, is it?" Tru asked.

"Yes?"

"I'd like for us to take a vacation together. Spend some of that quality time with each other that you shrinks are always talking about. I've got about four weeks' worth of overtime saved up. I really need a break. I was hoping you'd be interested in going with me. If I don't use it before the end of the year, I have to give it back to the city. I'd hate to give back for free what I've earned the hard way," Tru asserted.

"Where will we go? Do you like camping?" Marki asked hopefully. She'd been waiting what had seemed a long time to get Tru to herself, away from the caustic grind of police work.

"Does it come with room service?" Tru laughed as she watched surprise spread across Marki's face.

"You don't camp? Rugged little individualist like you and you don't like the great outdoors?" Marki teased.

"I don't camp very well. But I've only tried it a few times. I was very young, and all I can remember is snakes, insects, and a decided lack of hot showers." Tru frowned at the memory.

"It might be better this time. Or it might be another interesting adventure."

"We can talk about it. But I'd really rather have room service than another adventure right away," Tru complained.

"We'll see. In the meantime, why don't you and I go on a little early adventure of our own?" Marki suggested, rising from her chair and grasping Tru's hand.

"What do you have in mind?" Tru laughed lightly at the sultry look in Marki's eye.

"Wouldn't you like to know? Wouldn't you just like to know?" Marki responded as she led Tru back into the house.

A few of the publications of
THE NAIAD PRESS, INC.
P.O. Box 10543   Tallahassee, Florida 32302
Phone (850) 539-5965
Toll-Free Order Number: 1-800-533-1973
Mail orders welcome. Please include 15% postage.
Write or call for our free catalog which also features an
incredible selection of lesbian videos.

RHYTHM TIDE by Frankie J. Jones. 160 pp. . . . to desire
passionately and be passionately desired.   ISBN 1-56280-189-9 $11.95

PENN VALLEY PHOENIX by Janet McClellan. 208 pp. 2nd
Tru North Mystery.   ISBN 1-56280-200-3   11.95

BY RESERVATION ONLY by Jackie Calhoun. 240 pp. A
chance for true happiness.   ISBN 1-56280-191-0   11.95

OLD BLACK MAGIC by Jaye Maiman. 272 pp. 9th Robin
Miller Mystery.   ISBN 1-56280-175-9   11.95

LEGACY OF LOVE by Marianne K. Martin. 240 pp. Women
will do anything for her . . .   ISBN 1-56280-184-8   11.95

LETTING GO by Ann O'Leary. 160 pp. Laura, at 39, in love
with 23-year-old Kate.   ISBN 1-56280-183-X   11.95

LADY BE GOOD edited by Barbara Grier and Christine Cassidy.
288 pp. Erotic stories by Naiad Press authors.   ISBN 1-56280-180-5   14.95

CHAIN LETTER by Claire McNab. 288 pp. 9th Carol Ashton
mystery.   ISBN 1-56280-181-3   11.95

NIGHT VISION by Laura Adams. 256 pp. Erotic fantasy romance
by "famous" author.   ISBN 1-56280-182-1   11.95

SEA TO SHINING SEA by Lisa Shapiro. 256 pp. Unable to resist
the raging passion . . .   ISBN 1-56280-177-5   11.95

THIRD DEGREE by Kate Calloway. 224 pp. 3rd Cassidy James
mystery.   ISBN 1-56280-185-6   11.95

WHEN THE DANCING STOPS by Therese Szymanski. 272 pp.
1st Brett Higgins mystery.   ISBN 1-56280-186-4   11.95

PHASES OF THE MOON by Julia Watts. 192 pp. . . . . hungry
for everything life has to offer.   ISBN 1-56280-176-7   11.95

BABY IT'S COLD by Jaye Maiman. 256 pp. 5th Robin Miller
mystery.   ISBN 1-56280-156-2   10.95

CLASS REUNION by Linda Hill. 176 pp. The girl from her past . . .
ISBN 1-56280-178-3   11.95

DREAM LOVER by Lyn Denison. 224 pp. A soft, sensuous, romantic fantasy.
ISBN 1-56280-173-1   11.95

FORTY LOVE by Diana Simmonds. 288 pp. Joyous, heart-warming romance.
ISBN 1-56280-171-6   11.95

IN THE MOOD by Robbi Sommers. 160 pp. The queen of erotic tension!
ISBN 1-56280-172-4   11.95

SWIMMING CAT COVE by Lauren Douglas. 192 pp. 2nd Allison O'Neil Mystery.
ISBN 1-56280-168-6   11.95

THE LOVING LESBIAN by Claire McNab and Sharon Gedan. 240 pp. Explore the experiences that make lesbian love unique.
ISBN 1-56280-169-4   14.95

COURTED by Celia Cohen. 160 pp. Sparkling romantic encounter.
ISBN 1-56280-166-X   11.95

SEASONS OF THE HEART by Jackie Calhoun. 240 pp. Romance through the years.
ISBN 1-56280-167-8   11.95

K. C. BOMBER by Janet McClellan. 208 pp. 1st Tru North mystery.
ISBN 1-56280-157-0   11.95

LAST RITES by Tracey Richardson. 192 pp. 1st Stevie Houston mystery.
ISBN 1-56280-164-3   11.95

EMBRACE IN MOTION by Karin Kallmaker. 256 pp. A whirlwind love affair.
ISBN 1-56280-165-1   11.95

HOT CHECK by Peggy J. Herring. 192 pp. Will workaholic Alice fall for guitarist Ricky?
ISBN 1-56280-163-5   11.95

OLD TIES by Saxon Bennett. 176 pp. Can Cleo surrender to a passionate new love?
ISBN 1-56280-159-7   11.95

LOVE ON THE LINE by Laura DeHart Young. 176 pp. Will Stef win Kay's heart?
ISBN 1-56280-162-7   11.95

DEVIL'S LEG CROSSING by Kaye Davis. 192 pp. 1st Maris Middleton mystery.
ISBN 1-56280-158-9   11.95

COSTA BRAVA by Marta Balletbo Coll. 144 pp. Read the book, see the movie!
ISBN 1-56280-153-8   11.95

MEETING MAGDALENE & OTHER STORIES by Marilyn Freeman. 144 pp. Read the book, see the movie!
ISBN 1-56280-170-8   11.95

SECOND FIDDLE by Kate Calloway. 208 pp. P.I. Cassidy James' second case.
ISBN 1-56280-169-6   11.95

LAUREL by Isabel Miller. 128 pp. By the author of the beloved *Patience and Sarah*.
ISBN 1-56280-146-5   10.95

LOVE OR MONEY by Jackie Calhoun. 240 pp. The romance of real life.
ISBN 1-56280-147-3   10.95

SMOKE AND MIRRORS by Pat Welch. 224 pp. 5th Helen Black Mystery.
ISBN 1-56280-143-0   10.95

DANCING IN THE DARK edited by Barbara Grier & Christine Cassidy. 272 pp. Erotic love stories by Naiad Press authors.
ISBN 1-56280-144-9   14.95

TIME AND TIME AGAIN by Catherine Ennis. 176 pp. Passionate love affair.
ISBN 1-56280-145-7   10.95

PAXTON COURT by Diane Salvatore. 256 pp. Erotic and wickedly funny contemporary tale about the business of learning to live together.
ISBN 1-56280-114-7   10.95

INNER CIRCLE by Claire McNab. 208 pp. 8th Carol Ashton Mystery.
ISBN 1-56280-135-X   11.95

LESBIAN SEX: AN ORAL HISTORY by Susan Johnson. 240 pp. Need we say more?
ISBN 1-56280-142-2   14.95

WILD THINGS by Karin Kallmaker. 240 pp. By the undisputed mistress of lesbian romance.
ISBN 1-56280-139-2   11.95

THE GIRL NEXT DOOR by Mindy Kaplan. 208 pp. Just what you'd expect.
ISBN 1-56280-140-6   11.95

NOW AND THEN by Penny Hayes. 240 pp. Romance on the westward journey.
ISBN 1-56280-121-X   11.95

HEART ON FIRE by Diana Simmonds. 176 pp. The romantic and erotic rival of *Curious Wine*.
ISBN 1-56280-152-X   11.95

DEATH AT LAVENDER BAY by Lauren Wright Douglas. 208 pp. 1st Allison O'Neil Mystery.
ISBN 1-56280-085-X   11.95

YES I SAID YES I WILL by Judith McDaniel. 272 pp. Hot romance by famous author.
ISBN 1-56280-138-4   11.95

FORBIDDEN FIRES by Margaret C. Anderson. Edited by Mathilda Hills. 176 pp. Famous author's "unpublished" Lesbian romance.
ISBN 1-56280-123-6   21.95

SIDE TRACKS by Teresa Stores. 160 pp. Gender-bending Lesbians on the road.
ISBN 1-56280-122-8   10.95

HOODED MURDER by Annette Van Dyke. 176 pp. 1st Jessie Batelle Mystery.
ISBN 1-56280-134-1   10.95

WILDWOOD FLOWERS by Julia Watts. 208 pp. Hilarious and heart-warming tale of true love.
ISBN 1-56280-127-9   10.95

NEVER SAY NEVER by Linda Hill. 224 pp. Rule #1: Never get involved with . . .
ISBN 1-56280-126-0   11.95

THE SEARCH by Melanie McAllester. 240 pp. Exciting top cop Tenny Mendoza case.
ISBN 1-56280-150-3   10.95

THE WISH LIST by Saxon Bennett. 192 pp. Romance through the years.
ISBN 1-56280-125-2   10.95

FIRST IMPRESSIONS by Kate Calloway. 208 pp. P.I. Cassidy James' first case.
ISBN 1-56280-133-3   10.95

OUT OF THE NIGHT by Kris Bruyer. 192 pp. Spine-tingling
thriller. ISBN 1-56280-120-1   10.95

NORTHERN BLUE by Tracey Richardson. 224 pp. Police recruits
Miki & Miranda — passion in the line of fire. ISBN 1-56280-118-X   10.95

LOVE'S HARVEST by Peggy J. Herring. 176 pp. by the author of
Once More With Feeling. ISBN 1-56280-117-1   10.95

THE COLOR OF WINTER by Lisa Shapiro. 208 pp. Romantic
love beyond your wildest dreams. ISBN 1-56280-116-3   10.95

FAMILY SECRETS by Laura DeHart Young. 208 pp. Enthralling
romance and suspense. ISBN 1-56280-119-8   10.95

INLAND PASSAGE by Jane Rule. 288 pp. Tales exploring conven-
tional & unconventional relationships. ISBN 0-930044-56-8   10.95

DOUBLE BLUFF by Claire McNab. 208 pp. 7th Carol Ashton
Mystery. ISBN 1-56280-096-5   10.95

BAR GIRLS by Lauran Hoffman. 176 pp. See the movie, read
the book! ISBN 1-56280-115-5   10.95

THE FIRST TIME EVER edited by Barbara Grier & Christine
Cassidy. 272 pp. Love stories by Naiad Press authors.
ISBN 1-56280-086-8   14.95

MISS PETTIBONE AND MISS McGRAW by Brenda Weathers.
208 pp. A charming ghostly love story. ISBN 1-56280-151-1   10.95

CHANGES by Jackie Calhoun. 208 pp. Involved romance and
relationships. ISBN 1-56280-083-3   10.95

FAIR PLAY by Rose Beecham. 256 pp. 3rd Amanda Valentine
Mystery. ISBN 1-56280-081-7   10.95

PAYBACK by Celia Cohen. 176 pp. A gripping thriller of romance,
revenge and betrayal. ISBN 1-56280-084-1   10.95

THE BEACH AFFAIR by Barbara Johnson. 224 pp. Sizzling
summer romance/mystery/intrigue. ISBN 1-56280-090-6   10.95

GETTING THERE by Robbi Sommers. 192 pp. Nobody does it
like Robbi! ISBN 1-56280-099-X   10.95

FINAL CUT by Lisa Haddock. 208 pp. 2nd Carmen Ramirez
Mystery. ISBN 1-56280-088-4   10.95

FLASHPOINT by Katherine V. Forrest. 256 pp. A Lesbian
blockbuster! ISBN 1-56280-079-5   10.95

CLAIRE OF THE MOON by Nicole Conn. Audio Book —Read
by Marianne Hyatt. ISBN 1-56280-113-9   16.95

FOR LOVE AND FOR LIFE: INTIMATE PORTRAITS OF
LESBIAN COUPLES by Susan Johnson. 224 pp.
ISBN 1-56280-091-4   14.95

DEVOTION by Mindy Kaplan. 192 pp. See the movie — read
the book! ISBN 1-56280-093-0   10.95

SOMEONE TO WATCH by Jaye Maiman. 272 pp. 4th Robin
Miller Mystery.   ISBN 1-56280-095-7   10.95

GREENER THAN GRASS by Jennifer Fulton. 208 pp. A young
woman — a stranger in her bed.   ISBN 1-56280-092-2   10.95

TRAVELS WITH DIANA HUNTER by Regine Sands. Erotic
lesbian romp. Audio Book (2 cassettes)   ISBN 1-56280-107-4   16.95

CABIN FEVER by Carol Schmidt. 256 pp. Sizzling suspense
and passion.   ISBN 1-56280-089-1   10.95

THERE WILL BE NO GOODBYES by Laura DeHart Young. 192
pp. Romantic love, strength, and friendship.   ISBN 1-56280-103-1   10.95

FAULTLINE by Sheila Ortiz Taylor. 144 pp. Joyous comic
lesbian novel.   ISBN 1-56280-108-2   9.95

OPEN HOUSE by Pat Welch. 176 pp. 4th Helen Black Mystery.
                                            ISBN 1-56280-102-3   10.95

FOREVER by Evelyn Kennedy. 224 pp. Passionate romance — love
overcoming all obstacles.   ISBN 1-56280-094-9   10.95

WHISPERS by Kris Bruyer. 176 pp. Romantic ghost story
                                            ISBN 1-56280-082-5   10.95

NIGHT SONGS by Penny Mickelbury. 224 pp. 2nd Gianna
Maglione Mystery.   ISBN 1-56280-097-3   10.95

GETTING TO THE POINT by Teresa Stores. 256 pp. Classic
southern Lesbian novel.   ISBN 1-56280-100-7   10.95

PAINTED MOON by Karin Kallmaker. 224 pp. Delicious
Kallmaker romance.   ISBN 1-56280-075-2   11.95

THE MYSTERIOUS NAIAD edited by Katherine V. Forrest &
Barbara Grier. 320 pp. Love stories by Naiad Press authors.
                                            ISBN 1-56280-074-4   14.95

DAUGHTERS OF A CORAL DAWN by Katherine V. Forrest.
240 pp. Tenth Anniversay Edition.   ISBN 1-56280-104-X   11.95

  BODY GUARD by Claire McNab. 208 pp. 6th Carol Ashton
Mystery.   ISBN 1-56280-073-6   11.95

CACTUS LOVE by Lee Lynch. 192 pp. Stories by the beloved
storyteller.   ISBN 1-56280-071-X   9.95

These are just a few of the many Naiad Press titles — we are the oldest and
largest lesbian/feminist publishing company in the world. We also offer an
enormous selection of lesbian video products. Please request a complete
catalog. We offer personal service; we encourage and welcome direct mail
orders from individuals who have limited access to bookstores carrying our
publications.